THE
KABBALAH
MASTER

ALSO BY PERLE BESSERMAN

Novels and Collected Fiction

Kabuki Boy

Widow Zion

Yeshiva Girl

Nonfiction

Grassroots Zen

The Shambala Guide to Kabbalah and Jewish Mysticism

A New Kabbalah for Women

A New Zen for Women

Zen Radicals, Rebels, and Reformers

THE KABBALAH MASTER

a novel

Perle Besserman

Monkfish Book Publishing Company
Rhinebeck, NY

The Kabbalah Master: A Novel © 2018 by Perle Besserman

Cover design by Nita Ybarra.
Book design by Colin Rolfe.

Paperback ISBN: 978-1-939681-92-8
eBook ISBN: 978-1-939681-93-5

Library of Congress Cataloging-in-Publication Data

Names: Besserman, Perle, author.
Title: The Kabbalah master : a novel / Perle Besserman.
Description: Rhinebeck, NY : Monkfish Book Publishing Company, [2018]
Identifiers: LCCN 2018006419 (print) | LCCN 2017061375 (ebook) | ISBN
   9781939681935 (ebook) | ISBN 9781939681928 (softcover : acid-free paper)
Subjects: LCSH: Middle-aged women--Fiction. | Life change events--Fiction. |
   Jewish way of life--Fiction. | Jewish fiction.
Classification: LCC PS3602.E7829 (print) | LCC PS3602.E7829 K33 2018 (ebook)
   | DDC 813/.6--dc23
LC record available at https://lccn.loc.gov/2018006419

Monkfish Book Publishing Company
22 East Market Street, Suite 304
Rhinebeck, New York 12572
(845) 876-4861
www.monkfishpublishing.com

Through awe we come to love. ... There is only one degree more elevated than that of awe and that is love. Love contains the mystery of the unity of God. It is love that links the higher with the lower degrees; it is love that lifts everything to the level where all must become one.

—Rabbi Moses de Leon, from the Zohar

A woman can be proud and stiff
When on love intent
But Love has pitched his mansion in
The place of excrement...

—William Butler Yeats, from "Crazy Jane Talks With the Bishop"

For my brother Larry

ONE

I T WAS THE FIRST MONDAY AFTER THE FOURTH OF JULY, 1972. The Coney Island sky was overcast, the air gray, soft, and humid; the low-lying clouds fairly tumescent with rain. Hardly a day for a walk along the beach—an intermittent, fetid breeze from the water, where even the waves seemed to hang back, the ocean a stagnant pond of floating beer cans, ice cream wrappers, orange rinds, and a thousand and one other varieties of summer detritus from the city. The right day, the right time for purse snatchers, unemployed muscle builders, and those too frequent human hulks of indeterminate sex, clad to the eyes in their winter woolens, rag-puttees, and fingerless gloves poking around in the litter baskets flanking the boardwalk's few open food stands. Certainly not the kind of day Sharon normally would have chosen for such an outing—not after working without sleep from the Sabbath sundown straight through to Monday morning at five in her hot, cramped cubbyhole with the small desk fan that she dared not use for fear of scattering to the winds Rabbi Joachim's precious Kabbalistic notes, secret mystical formulas that were too powerful to trust to the typewriter and had to be copied by hand. Still, though she was bone-tired, Sharon had deliberately chosen not to return home after work, but to walk—after a breakfast of three cups of black coffee and nothing else all day—to the beach instead. The rabbi had kindly offered to drive her home, but Sharon had refused. Spending two days alone with him, helping to extricate the rainbow emanations of his faith from the black morass of ancient Hebrew letters and mystic symbols bequeathed to him by a long line of Kabbalists was hard enough. And then, beyond that, silently loving him, straining to control the forbidden urges of her flesh whenever he leaned over her shoulder and grazed her arm with the lapel of his jacket, not daring to steal so much as a glimpse of his averted eyes. As an Orthodox married man, Rabbi Joachim was pro-hibited from looking directly upon the face of any woman other than his wife or, for that matter, working alone with a woman in his tiny office. But he was a Kabbalah master, and Kabbalah masters had their own way of being Orthodox—like his lineage of Lithuanian Hasidic saints known for their capacious healing powers and frequent run-ins with the rationalists in the traditional rabbinic establishment. A dap-per modern cleric in his fifties who'd been a dentist before consenting to the growing call of the Lord, the rabbi was reputed to be a happily married father of two boys and an infant daughter. In his dark, tailored suits and rakishly angled slouch hats, he was certainly not "rabbinic looking"—hardly a candidate for mystical visions or, Sharon thought as she sat down on a broken bench facing the beach, the sensitive and tender kind of man she'd been fantasizing about since her divorce from her clodhopper husband Barney.

Feeling isolated and curious about the growing popularity of spir-itual practices available since the late Sixties, she'd joined a yoga class where she met a group of women "spiritual seekers." It was Malina, the leader of the group, who'd invited her to attend one of the rabbi's public lectures on the Kabbalistic Path to Self-Knowledge. Seated in the front row and twice receiving his enigmatic, grace-bestowing smile, she'd become an instant devotee. As the lecture ended and the audience was lining up at the table in front of the dais to enroll in Rabbi Joachim's Center for Mystical Judaism, Malina pushed her forward. "Wow, Sharon, did you see how he picked you out from the crowd? You two must have a strong karmic connection!" Thrilled at having caught the rabbi's eye and being somehow special, Sharon had immediately signed up as a member. With her enthusiasm for the mysteries of the Kabbalah enhanced by Rabbi Joachim's continuing attention, she'd abandoned her yoga classes and become a regular at the Center, religiously attending his every seminar and workshop, and remaining afterward to erase the blackboard and turn out the lights. Within a year, she'd graduated from these simple chores to become his secretary. By then, having lost their taste for the Kabbalah, her friend Malina and the original group of women spiritual seekers had moved on to Tibetan Buddhism, never to be heard from again.

It was hotter now that a milky sun had parted the cloud cover and was blazing down on the flat, open expanse of the boardwalk. Behind her, an occasional blast of music wafted from the depths of a stand where a man in a chef's toque was selling popcorn and cotton candy. Coney Island, a festering wound on the leg of the city—most of it boarded up now, even the Whip. How she'd loved that wild, electric ride as a child; her head snapping forward to the terrifying false starts engineered by the pimpled teenager working the switches. That boy in the dark blue, sleeveless t-shirt, had tormented the screaming riders with the promise of speed, waiting until he'd wrung their last shred of patience and only then throwing the magic lever, setting them all on a collision course, crashing head-on, whirling in every direction across the spark-crackling steel floor.

Sharon pushed off one shoe and dangled it from her big toe. Her life had been a lot like riding the Whip, the denied promise of pleasure providing an odd little island of pleasure all its own—inexplicably leading to her as yet unrequited love for her mentor. And something, of course, to do with the fact that Rabbi Joachim had steered her out of a spiritual blind alley into the radiant light of the sages and committed her to "God's greater cause."

Should she slip off both shoes? A modest Jewish woman, the secretary to the president of the Center for Mystical Judaism, did not go barefoot in public. Briefly wiggling her toes, she slid her foot back into the shoe. God, it was hot. She could feel the sweat coursing down in streams under the arms of her long-sleeved white blouse, her heavy black weskit sticking to her ribs like the mustard plasters her mother would stick on her chest at the slightest sign of a sniffle when she was a kid. Impulsively, Sharon laid aside her purse, quickly unsnapped the weskit, pulled it off, and kicked off both shoes.

Pinnie would be angry with her for not coming right home. She'd complain for hours about the terrible habits of the children: "Paulie ate Fritos for lunch again, Sharon. You know, his teeth are getting black from all the candy he shoves into his mouth. If you don't watch out, he'll be smoking before you can turn your head around. And you should only hear the language he uses with me! From a yeshiva boy, yet! He talks more like a truck driver than an eleven-year-old boy from a religious family. And Phyllis, poor little doll, she misses you so much she hardly eats at all."

Whenever Pinnie mentioned Phyllis, she would place her index finger on her cheek and her thumb on her chin, an inadvertent gesture betraying her preference for her compliant granddaughter over her unruly grandson.

"She cries, 'When is my Mommy coming home?' all day and all

night. And she's right, God bless her. Who in her right mind leaves a little girl alone like that?"

"But you're with them, Pinnie," Sharon would answer. "You're the beloved grandma who wipes their noses and lives here rent-free while their big, bad Mommy has to go out and earn the money to buy them Fritos."

Then Sharon would turn away from her mother and go off to brood, or sleep, resolving to call Barney, her ex, the next day and plead with him to send the alimony check on time because she was down to seventy-five cents by mid-month and the landlady downstairs was not exactly threatening but was giving her a certain mid-month look which meant the kids wouldn't be sharing the big rubber pool in the yard. But invariably, she would *not* call Barney after all, but would walk to Coney Island instead, and sit on the same bench on the boardwalk in front of the shuttered building where the ghostly echo of the Whip had lured her with its childhood promise of denied pleasure.

Pinnie would have a fit if she could see her now, sprawled out on the bench, fair-skinned and hatless, inviting sunstroke in the furious, damp heat of noon, her weskit flung down beside her, her purse carelessly tossed on top of the weskit. Out on the water, the flat-snout prow of a tanker pierced the haze, and a few feet away from where she sat, the Parachute ascended and disappeared into the clouds, leaving behind a fragile trail of half-hearted screams from the girlfriends of sailors on leave.

Why couldn't Barney cooperate and send the alimony on time just this once—as a birthday present to her? Her birthday was next week, her thirty-fifth already—her life seemed to be careening past her on the nerve-mangling iron wheels of the eternal Whip. How old could the Rebbitzen Joachim be? Twenty-six? Thirty-two? Rumor had it that Rabbi Joachim had been married late, to a much younger woman. Sharon had never met the Rebbitzen. Had the rabbi, for that matter, ever again mentioned his wife after answering Sharon's one tentative question about his family? Not that she could recall. "My wife and children live in Israel, Mrs. Berg, where one day, with God's help, I plan to move the Center entirely," he had said. After that curt dismissal, emphasizing the singular *I*, there had been no further talk of his wife and children, and Sharon retreated into embarrassed silence.

She allowed herself to stew in the heat. She could always quit her job and never see Rabbi Joachim again, try working at the library instead. Or maybe not, since you needed a degree in library science, and she only had a secretarial school certificate. Her father, a prolific reader and magnetizing storyteller, had taught her to read when she was four. Sharon had always loved the library, since she was a kid, and visited it often, proudly coming home with her arms filled with books. Then her father had died and she'd gotten married and stopped reading—stopped everything. Still, heeding Pinnie's folksy advice had worked once before, with Barney: "If you have your health and your years"—that was her mother's way of saying *youth*—"you can just pick up and start again no matter how dark it looks to you." Fed up with her husband's television addiction, his dandruff, and his grunts for "good morning," "good night," and "I love you," Sharon had packed up without warning, moved herself and the kids to a new apartment, enrolled in a six-week shorthand refresher course, and, after retrieving her mother from her widow's canasta circuit, resumed living. Well, at least she had resumed a *way* of living that was far more bearable even in its loneliness than exile in the company of a slug. After years of toying with the idea of divorce and thrusting it aside at the prospect of foundering alone "out there" as a single mother, she knew she could not trade security with Barney for her freedom. In the end, it had been her determination to carve out her very own special slice of life for herself that had carried her through.

Suddenly a man sat down at the other end of the bench. Sharon quickly slipped her feet back into her shoes, pulled on her weskit, and set her purse in her lap. The man looked harmless enough, and disinterested, but you could never tell. Not that she had any money in her purse to speak of—there was less than five dollars left after yesterday's grocery shopping. Harry, the Center's accountant, sent her paycheck to her direct deposit account at the bank every month and she'd hidden her credit cards in a drawer after her divorce, so there wasn't much worth stealing in her wallet. But there were personal things there, irreplaceable things, including a lock of Phyllis's golden baby hair squeezed into a plastic folder that also contained a precious faded snapshot of her father as a young man, standing arms akimbo against a sepia Prospect Park tree, his dark, curly hair worn long over his forehead, gazing out of the photograph with the same look of failed ambition in his eyes Sharon had inherited; a religious talisman inscribed with blessings for health and fortune given her at the Center's orientation ceremony; a red thread to protect her against the evil eye; her Social Security card; and a free, still unused movie pass for two. She decided to sit just a few minutes longer so as not to give her bench mate the impression that she was afraid of him. Only the very brave and the very crazy took to the benches of Coney Island alone these days. Sharon could hear Pinnie's chastising voice: "You take your life in your hands when you go to sit on the Boardwalk."

Clutching her purse, Sharon stole a stealthy glance at the man sitting at the other end of the bench. He looked to be in his late twenties, and was rather swarthy, wearing a pink dress shirt open down to the breast bone. His bare chest was brown and hairless at the V of the shirt's opening, and he wore a heavy ivory skull with fake ruby-studded eye sockets hanging from a long silver chain. He had a handsome sort of face—if you cared for the Warren Beatty type—the same regular features, square chin, blue eyes, and shock of dark hair. From the little that Sharon could see without turning to face him or moving closer, he'd taken up a pad and pencil and begun sketching. Every so often he would look up from the pad toward the beach, but not at her. Well, thank God for that.

The screams coming from the descending Parachute were louder now. She would count to two hundred and fifty and then leave. She'd stewed in the heat long enough for today; tomorrow she would go back to work again, taking Rabbi Joachim's dictation on the seventeen variations of the Holy Name. After only a short while the sun had purged her of her desire for the rabbi to place his mouth on her ear as she called out the numbers at the upper right-hand corner of the coding cards. What would she do come autumn and winter if this insanity persisted? The winter cold might freeze her passion. But the crisp and lovely days of autumn, when her body was more dangerously alive than ever—what then? Autumn was only two short months away. Hopefully the rabbi would be visiting his family in Israel. If fate was kind to her, she might even meet someone new by then. (She hadn't been touched by a man for over a year.) Then again, if she persisted in wandering around Coney Island alone after the summer ended, she might be mugged, beaten, or even raped and murdered, her body discarded under the boardwalk, like that woman whose hideously decaying corpse had been featured on the front page of *The New York Post* less than a year ago.

Sharon mentally counted the passing seconds: two hundred and thirty-nine, two hundred and forty—she was unbearably hot and thirsty now, even a little dizzy. The thought of a pitcher of lemonade in the refrigerator at home urged her on. She counted faster: two hundred and forty-one, two hundred and forty-two. Sharon had reached two hundred and forty-seven when a gang of young men materialized seemingly out of nowhere and approached the bench mumbling a barrage of Spanish curses.

"Hey, Baybeeee," their leader addressed her loudly in English, "I wanna ast you a question!" He was about nineteen, short and round as a beer cask, bare-chested and wearing oversized surfer shorts, high-top basketball sneakers, and a black wool beanie on his head. In addition to the leader, there were four similarly dressed bare-chested young men now clustered around her, one of them carrying a baseball glove. Frantically looking around for the accompanying bat, Sharon was so relieved at not seeing one that she almost burst out laughing. Still, the incongruous combination of basketball sneakers and baseball glove frightened her. Only a week before, over lunch at the Chelsea Bagel Shop, gazing at her through purple-tinted cat-eye glasses, Sharon's streetwise sister Arleen had warned, "You know those high-top basketball sneakers those gang members wear? They're not just a fashion statement. They wear them so they can run away at top speed after they've mugged you, the bastards."

Still sketching, the man sitting next to her on the bench shifted closer. Sharon mutely implored his help. With none forthcoming, she began to panic. What if he didn't understand English? Worse yet, what if he was one of those perverts who got his kicks from watching a woman being gang-raped? A Niagara of terror coursed through Sharon's bloodstream as, unable to move, she sat pondering the grisly options. It did not, oddly enough, occur to her to mentally recite the Kabbalistic chant Rabbi Joachim had taught her for protection in times of danger.

"Hey, Baybeee, I wanna ast yuh this question," the barrel-chested gang leader taunted again.

A burst of hoots and whistles erupted behind him. Seeing that Sharon wasn't going to put up a fight, his companions were growing restless.

"Come on!" A taller young man with the dark hint of a mustache placed his hand on the leader's shoulder.

"Git yuh hands offa me, Paulie," Barrel Chest tossed his friend aside with one violent sweep of his palm and Paulie, now embarrassed, hung back. He had the same name as her son. This was no coincidence. Hadn't Rabbi Joachim told her there was no such thing as coincidence, that everything was part of God's heavenly plan— even evil? What was happening to her now was no better than she deserved. She was being punished for neglecting her own Paulie who, at eleven, was already cursing his way into the downward path of his namesake, the "Paulie" who stood threatening her at that very moment.

"Look, why don't you just go away? I don't want to hear your question. Go home." Sharon startled herself with the calm strength of her own voice.

"Huh?" Barrel Chest rolled his eyes, pretending to be shocked.

If the Hebrew letters were truly living entities quivering with divine power, then uttering God's secret Name would instantly vaporize Barrel Chest and his gang. "The Tetragrammaton is the most powerful creative force in all of Nature. Yet at the same time, it can be more destructive than the atom bomb!" Rabbi Joachim had thundered, swinging his fist over her head like a censer. Was it because she was still only a novice or because she was a woman that he had never revealed the secret Name and delivered its power to her?

"Listen, Baybeee," Barrel Chest said, edging closer, "I got this very important question I gotta ast yuh."

Sharon raged inwardly at her powerlessness.

Well, ask it then, you punk! Why the long prologue? Go on and ask me if I dropped my handkerchief. And when I say no, tell me you don't care if I bleed to death. Or are you going to make some disgusting sucking

*noise and ask me to give you a blowjob under the boardwalk? Will you
and your gang of Paulies run off laughing and cursing in Spanish after
fondling my breasts while Pretty Boy sits here drawing sea gulls?*

As if in direct response to her unspoken challenge, the man sitting
next to her called out, "Hey, guys, why don't you leave the lady alone?"

Eyes flaming, Barrel Chest turned to face him. Sharon thought
of making a run for the stand where the man in the chef's toque was
now cleaning up and preparing to leave. But the other gang members,
piqued by the prospect of a fight, had massed even closer to the bench,
pinning her in.

"Hey, man, you must be Arnold Schwarzenegger? Did you hear
that, boys, we got us Mr. Olympia himself on this here bench?" mocked
the smallest gang member.

Paulie spat and offered him a high five.

"Shut up!" ordered their leader.

Suddenly everything came to a standstill. The Parachute, too, Sharon noticed, was oddly suspended in midair. Had it been stopped by
her merely thinking of the Holy Name? Or had time itself stopped,
the way it did when the rabbi flew through the streets in his red Volvo
without the cops noticing? The panicked girls clinging to their sailor
boyfriends in the stalled gondola think *they're* the ones in danger, Sharon mused. To them, I'm lucky to be safely on the ground. Funny, how
it's all a matter of perspective.

"Do you know this lady, man?" Barrel Chest said in a low, menacing tone to the man sitting next to her. Still, there was a trace of humor
in his eyes. Or was she misjudging, finding humor when it was mania
that had turned the gang leader's darting gaze into a pair of flaming
pinwheels?

"Yes," the stranger answered pleasantly.

"Is she yuh wife, man? Otherwise, I mean, if she ain't yuh wife, yuh know, yuh gotta mind yuh own business. Yuh know what I mean, man?" Barrel Chest finished almost in a whisper.

Sharon's bench mate smiled at her—a perfect, straight white-toothed smile in what she now saw was a startlingly handsome face.

The thugs released a communal chuckle.

"Shut up!" screamed Barrel Chest, this time without turning to face them. Sharon watched the sweat pour in dual tracks along his temples. A vein formed a purple arrow in his forehead. His body was trembling with the effort to withhold the rage that she imagined mobilized him, woke him each morning, and thrust him into the streets, compelling his fists to slam against flesh. Turning squarely toward the man on the bench he demanded, "Ansuh me loud now, man, 'cuz I ain't gonna ast you again—you this lady's husband?"

"Yes, I'm her husband," was the instant reply.

"That's funny, that's really funny, man," the leader addressed his companions over his shoulder. "Did you hear that, you muthas, this dude's her husband?" Then, turning to Sharon, he asked, "Lady is this really yuh husband?"

Sharon tried to accompany her short nod with a timid smile, which only served to infuriate her interrogator further. The humorous gleam in his eye had disappeared entirely.

"Then why yuh sittin' so far apart? If yuz is married, why yuh sittin' at opposite ends of the bench?" Without waiting for an answer, the gang leader smacked his right fist into his open left palm and again, barely above a whisper, addressed the man on the bench: "Yuh sure yuh not lyin' to me, man?"

"No, I'm not lying," replied the stranger, this time only almost cheerfully. "I draw and she likes to sit and look at the water and think, so we sit far apart—"

"That the truth, lady?"

"Yes."

"Let's see whut yuh drawin' now, man."

The Parachute slumped, creaked, seemed almost to stumble from its moorings, and at last groaned its way earthward. Meanwhile, Barrel Chest, the master of chaos, approached the stranger while his entourage of lesser fiends, once again visibly impatient, rustled behind him. "Paulie," the favored one—could he be the leader's conscience-plagued brother, Sharon wondered—pressed forward pleading softly: "Come on, man. We not gonna beat on this mutha five against one. He's one of them artist faggots, man. Like, we ain't gonna bother to beat on 'im, are we?"

This time the gang leader did not even bother to push Paulie away. Every particle of Barrel Chest's attention was now focused on the sketchpad.

"Let's see what yuh draw, man."

Sharon felt her leg muscles turn to batter. Amiably, the artist handed over his sketchpad.

The gang grouped in closer around their leader for a look.

"This ain't no picture, this is gahbage, man, gahbage!" the tormentor screamed, pulling the sketch pad out of the artist's hands and holding it high over his head.

"Hey, man, give the faggot back his pad and let's split, man. We all ain't gonna beat on 'im, right, man?" Paulie persisted, now bolstered by short bursts of assent from the others.

Suddenly, Barrel Chest appeared to be seized by a cramp and on the verge of collapsing. He hunched his body in two and flung down the pad at the artist's feet. Saliva bubbling at the corners of his mouth, he backed away, shrieking, "I fought over in Vietnam, killed me plenty of mutha fuckas like you! Don't wanna hear none uh yuh faggot artist mutha fuckas tellin' me what to do, hear me, man? Sure she's yuh wife, man—don't yuh tell me, yuh lyin' mutha fucka!" Signaling his gang to follow him, the leader sprang in front of Sharon, snatched her purse, and fled with it down to the beach.

The next thing Sharon knew she was running on the sand behind her bench mate, who had barely introduced himself to her as "Junior Cantana" before leaping up and chasing after the thief. Finding it impossible to run in her shoes, she took them off and carried them as she headed toward the water's edge, where the tide had flattened the sand. The gang had dispersed, leaving only their leader running ahead with her purse, twirling it around by the strap. Every so often he would tease her, pretending to return the purse to her before pulling it back and bellowing, "Come and get it, lady!"

The sun emerged briefly, but retreated just as quickly. Sharon's legs were cramping. At one point she feared they were buckling under her. At last, unable to go forward, ready to concede victory to her tormentor, she dropped to the sand. Shading her eyes, she saw Junior Cantana closing in on the thief. Now he was almost close enough to reach out and touch the corner of her purse. But the thief drew it back again. Together they circled, rose to a clinch that never materialized, and panting, feinted like boxers. An acrid breeze smelling of diesel fuel billowed out her rescuer's pink shirt in back. Sharon remained seated at the water's edge, numbly watching the two men.

"Yuh—wan—this—bag—man?" screamed the panting tormentor, "Come—and—get—it!" Then, without warning, he dropped the purse onto the sand in front of him.

Junior Cantana moved in closer.

An old woman in a faded blue bathing suit and sneakers came out of the water and walked between them. "Bums, that's all you get on the beach here lately is bums," she muttered.

Sharon was close enough to see the muscles tense in the old woman's face. She wanted to get up and run for help but could not lift herself from the sand. "Please, oh, please, call the police," she screamed, but the old woman waddled past, ignoring her.

At that moment, Junior Cantana sprang forward, thrust out his left leg and drove one swift karate kick to the tormentor's stomach. Stunned, the thief burst into tears and fell down on the sand.

"I—was—in—the—military—in—Vietnam, too," Junior Cantana panted, gathering up Sharon's purse and his sketch pad in one motion. "Are you feeling healthy enough to get up and walk over to the police station, or do I have to carry you there?"

The tormentor hid his face in his hands and sobbed. By that time Sharon had regained her ability to move and was sobbing too.

* * *

As it turned out, the gang leader, whose name was Jorge Diaz, had never been to Vietnam. He'd never finished basic training in South Carolina, where he'd first been introduced to pep pills and then graduated to heroin and a dishonorable discharge. According to Edward Pols, the arresting officer at the Coney Island precinct, Jorge was no teenager, either—"just a baby-faced twenty-three-year-old punk."

On the other hand, the man who identified himself as Specialist Fourth Class Carlo Gianni Cantana had served for eighteen months in Vietnam before being wounded in the stomach and sent back home. A recuperating soldier on leave—Sharon marveled at the irony of it. Imagine, she thought, as she signed her name under Carlo Gianni Cantana's in the charge book, me being saved from a junkie by a karate freak fighting a war I don't believe in.

It took over half an hour to book Diaz, who sat nodding on a bench throughout the proceedings. Handcuffed and surrounded by police-men, he was no longer menacing but looked pathetic. The sympathetic desk sergeant warned Sharon that a trial would be time consuming but it was the only way to get Jorge Diaz into rehab. Otherwise, he'd no doubt be on the street again the next day snatching some other woman's purse—or maybe even dead of an overdose on a tenement rooftop in Spanish Harlem. Prodded by generations of Jewish identification with the underdog, Sharon agreed to take the case to court. She would be informed of the date by mail, the desk sergeant said. Edward Pols would accompany her as the arresting officer. Without being asked, Carlo Gianni Cantana volunteered to testify on her behalf.

TWO

SHARON SECRETLY HOPED that what she had come to think of as "the boardwalk incident" would magically change her life for the better. But it did not. At home, her run-ins with her mother continued; in fact, they seemed to increase. The tension between them rose to such a pitch one night that Pinnie threatened to take the children away with her to the country for the rest of the summer if Sharon didn't "stop mooning over that rabbi and start acting like a mother again." In an attempt to divert her anger from her mother, Sharon went downstairs and got into a foolish argument with the landlady over a leak in the bathtub instead.

"People who don't pay their rent on time shouldn't complain so much about the plumbing!" the landlady shouted from the porch within earshot of the surrounding neighbors.

Pinnie was furious. "Now everyone on Westminster Road knows that Sharon Berg doesn't pay the rent on time. That witch! I tell you, Sharon, if you don't call that pig of an ex-husband of yours and tell him to send the money tonight, *I* will."

Resenting Pinnie's habit of using Barney and the children as an excuse for probing into her private life, Sharon had long stopped confiding in her. Besides, these days she was working from morning to midnight and she had no time to talk to her mother even if she'd wanted to. The raise Rabbi Joachim had promised her had never come through, but, not wanting him to think she was more interested in money than in being his disciple, she had been too ashamed to remind him of it.

Except that she no longer went to the beach to sit on her bench and dream, nothing had changed. No matter, her work at the Center now kept her from dreaming at all. Immediately after completing his index of variations on the Holy Name, Rabbi Joachim had plunged into research on a new "secret project." He was, in fact, so preoccupied with it that Sharon—whose job it was to clear up the odds and ends of the old and prepare the way for the new—hardly found herself at home.

Even after a year of working so closely with Rabbi Joachim, she could still marvel at the inexhaustible draughts of energy he seemed to draw from some hidden mystical source. No sooner would he complete one enormous task than he was already embarked on another, leaving Sharon struggling not to fall behind. What made it harder was that he never really explained anything. Only once had he stopped in the middle of describing the intricate network of *Sephiroth* on the mystical Tree of Life to recount his own experience in Jerusalem as an adept of his uncle, a Kabbalah master noted for eating no meat, drinking no wine, and living in hermetic celibacy.

"It was this holy man, my master, whom I watched as he single-handedly foiled the Arabs during the Six-Day War," the rabbi recalled. Holding his hands out in front of him in a gesture of benediction, his voice rising slightly, he recreated the event for Sharon.

"Like this, he stood on a Jerusalem hilltop overlooking the city. The sky was suddenly filled with clouds. Even the birds grew still. All we could hear was the distant rattle of gunfire in the valley below us. Turning his gaze toward heaven, my master suddenly cried out in a voice like thunder: '*Shema Yisroel Adonai Eloheinu Adonai echad!*' A streak of lightning pierced the sky. The gunfire seemed to draw closer. Suddenly I heard shouting, men's voices swelling louder and louder, coming closer and closer to the city. I looked at my master's face. His eyes were closed and his cheeks were bathed in tears. Afraid of what might happen if I addressed him, I crept away softly and made my way back to the three-room schoolhouse where I had lived and studied and prayed under his guidance since the beginning of the war. My body was limp. Sweating and chilled at once, drained of the psychic power he had drawn from me in order to reinforce the spell I stumbled blindly into my hammock and fell into a deep, trancelike sleep. That night I awoke to the mingled sounds of mourning and rejoicing. After centuries, Jerusalem was ours again! The war was over."

The Rabbi paused; then, almost in a whisper, he resumed. "But my master was dead. He had given his life in exchange for the life of Israel." Rolling the sensuous last *r* across his tongue, the Rabbi fell silent.

Overcome by love and vicarious religious ecstasy, Sharon choked down a sob.

As always, after delivering one of his "exempla," Rabbi Joachim recovered himself by brushing his hand over his silky black goatee and blinking the tears from his eyes. Within seconds, and with seemingly no effort, his voice and appearance returned from the exalted realms to the everyday reality of the Center's cramped little office.

The spiritual high and its precipitous drop left Sharon confused. Rabbi Joachim's uncle's momentous self-sacrifice contradicted everything he had told her about the Jewish prohibition against martyrdom. Hoping that he would eventually reveal the story's deeper meaning to her as she matured in her practice of Kabbalah, she refrained from pointing this out. Like the color charts depicting the complexities of the cosmic spheres, this mysterious parable would have to be shelved until she was ready to grasp it. Right now, her task as a devoted disciple was to stay open to Rabbi Joachim's teaching by following his instructions for clearing her mind and concentrating on the Holy Name. As a woman irrationally in love with a married man, who also happened to be her employer, she was less certain of their relationship. Admittedly, she'd had little interest in religion before attending his lecture that first night. Her grandmother had meticulously observed the ceremonies of the faith—lighting candles every Friday evening at sunset, dropping pennies into the blue-and-white charity box on the refrigerator, taking her to the synagogue on the High Holidays. But her grandmother's orthodoxy had died with her, and the remainder of Sharon's adolescence had been loosely governed by Pinnie's earthy agnosticism. Perhaps the fact that there were no men in her family, since both her grandfathers and her father had died young, had something to do with it—Judaism being such a male-centered religion. Maybe if her father hadn't left a house full of women adrift, she'd have been less prone to spiritual searching. Perhaps then she would have been contented with the life of an ordinary Jewish woman. It would have been enough for her to have membership in a suburban sisterhood, a prosperous religious book salesman for a husband, a son who did not curse and hit his grandmother when she told him to go to bed—or at least Sharon would have then had the money to pay for psychological counseling. But that wasn't her fate.

Unlike her sister Arleen, Sharon hadn't left home, taking off from Brooklyn for Manhattan, claiming she was an artist and needed space to work in, Arleen had declared her independence by living in a cold-water loft on the Lower East Side, with nothing but a mattress on the floor to sleep on. But even if Sharon had been lucky enough to paint or write, or daring enough to model nude for her rebellious younger sister and her artist friends, she would have somehow managed to remain closer to home. It was ironic. Here she was, having married in her twenties and divorced in her early thirties, living with her mother as the good daughter, the "normal" one whose marriage had simply come off badly—a fact of life that even middle-class Brooklyn modern orthodox Jews no longer frowned upon. Yet hadn't Sharon truly strayed as far away from home in spirit as Arleen had in the flesh? Hadn't her grandmother left her mark, imprinting her with a craving to appease an underlying hunger to penetrate the mysteries of what white-haired Bubbe Clara had called "the next world?"

* * *

RABBI JOACHIM DID NOT CHOOSE to disclose the particulars of his secret new project until every envelope containing the lists for his work on the Holy Name had been sealed and sent off to Israel. Carting them in a mailbag in a wheeled wire basket to the Post Office, Sharon had delivered the lot as instructed. There, scholars at the original Center for Mystical Judaism—the one founded by the disciples of Rabbi Joachim's late uncle—would collate the material and print it as a soft-covered book in a limited Hebrew edition to be followed six months later by another, in English. It was a clumsy procedure and, because of the distance and the language difficulties they'd encountered, fraught with misunderstandings that had delayed publication. Still, notwithstanding all the hardships, their total dependence on donations from wealthy disciples, and the assistance of a theosophical book publisher, Rabbi Joachim's increasing American success had resulted in the publication of three newly translated English editions of three fifteenth-century Aramaic Kabbalah manuscripts within one year. Modestly, the rabbi had claimed no credit for himself, ascribing the success of the enterprise to the intervention of his late uncle's spirit. Except for one whimsical reference to "smuggling photocopies out of the Vatican Library like an espionage agent," which Sharon had taken as one of the rabbi's rare attempts at a joke, he remained dead serious about his uncle's ongoing participation in the Center's affairs. Curious, since he'd never mentioned it, Sharon had asked if his master was a traditional rabbi before becoming a Kabbalist.

"Not *was*, Sharon—*IS!*" he exclaimed. "You must understand that although you cannot see him embodied in flesh, he is as close to you now, in this very room, as I am. When we speak of a spirit like his, there is no death," he continued peevishly, glaring at her. Then, softening a bit, putting his hand to his temple as if chastising himself for his impatience: "But forgive me, Sharon. How could you understand this? You are so young yet; someday the clouds of illusion will disappear for you, too, you'll see." That was the first time Rabbi Joachim had called her "Sharon," and the first time she had a dream about him that turned out to be a premonition.

* * *

THE NEW PROJECT, THE RABBI EXPLAINED, could not be described there in the office. To really understand what it was all about, they needed to drive to New Jersey and experience it firsthand. Afterward, there would be scheduled appointments, first with the Center's theosophical Delancey Street publisher, and next, if time allowed, with an herbalist in the neighborhood.

Sharon was intrigued, and happy to be quitting the office. The telephone hadn't stopped ringing and filling the morning with bad news: Leon Berkowitz, one of their most generous donors, in the process of searching for a building in which to relocate the Center, had scouted properties in a dangerous neighborhood and been mugged and robbed of three-hundred dollars and was recuperating from a fractured knee at Lenox Hill Hospital, and a shipment of explanatory brochures addressed to a Reform Temple in Orlando, Florida, had come back from the post office marked *Insufficient Postage.*

Thus it was that Sharon found herself—like in her dream—sitting alongside Rabbi Joachim driving through the midday muck of the Holland Tunnel. An elderly patron had rethought her will and at the last minute, transferred ownership of her car to the Center: a big red Volvo sedan with cream-colored leather seats and matching carpet throughout. Rabbi Joachim was unfazed by the flashy luxuriousness of the car. After uttering a short prayer of thanks to the generous intervention of his uncle, he'd sprung behind the wheel and driven off, screeching to a stop at red lights, narrowly avoiding rear ending the cars in front of him. Nothing fazed him out on the road, either—not the grizzled truck drivers looking down and cursing at him from their cabs, nor the startled pedestrians who jumped back onto the curbs swinging their fists in his wake. Safely wrapped in the spiritual embrace of his miracle-working uncle, Rabbi Joachim remained oblivious to their curses.

The traffic broke as they sped out of the tunnel onto the ramp and climbed toward the Palisades Parkway. The heavy, rainless humidity plaguing the city had turned into a thick haze blanketing the Manhattan skyline, making it almost invisible from the New Jersey side of the Hudson. The Palisades Parkway was eerily empty. For ten minutes they drove north, passed only by one other car—a state trooper, as it turned out, who seemed oddly unaware of the speeding red Volvo. Suppressing the urge to warn the rabbi that the trooper might be planning to pull him over and ticket him for speeding, Sharon focused instead on the direction they were taking. About half a mile from the Nyack exit, Rabbi Joachim pulled the car onto the grass shoulder, where a sign informed him it was illegal to park. Motioning for her to follow him, he opened the door of the car, and after removing his jacket and throwing it on the front seat, got out and strode briskly toward the Palisade cliffs. Following behind, Sharon assessed the rabbi's body as he plodded along like a bear looking neither left nor right. For a man who ate so little, he was broad and lumpy. Yet, seeing him out in the open, wearing his usual old-fashioned, white-on-white shirt with the pen-filled pockets and gold cufflinks, only made Sharon desire him more.

The grass closer to the river was wet and high. Sharon gazed at the emptiness around her and wondered where her mentor could be heading to with such determination. She was too busy looking around to notice that the terrain had dipped, allowing Rabbi Joachim to suddenly disappear from view. Hampered by her thick-heeled shoes, and at the same time curious, she pushed forward.

"Here—here it is!" she heard him call just as she caught sight of the top of his head.

Rabbi Joachim had taken off his hat and was kneeling near a very large boulder, one end of which protruded steeply over the river, the other flattened benignly against a plateau.

Sharon was struck by a surge of panic. What was she doing here? Was it because her life with Barney had been so irritably sane? Was that the reason she was perched insanely behind Rabbi Joachim on the New Jersey Palisades on a steamy Wednesday afternoon in July? Had he sensed enough of her own hidden madness to bring her here in the first place? What cosmic lesson was the rabbi trying to teach her this time?

"Here—here is the plant I've been looking for," he called out. "I knew I remembered the spot. Come, Sharon, quickly, we're running out of time."

"Where, Rabbi? I don't think I can make it down there with these shoes," she protested.

Since it was not Rabbi Joachim's habit to indulge her questions, Sharon wasn't surprised when he ignored her now. Even in the best of circumstance it wasn't unusual for him to maintain long stretches of silence before acknowledging her presence at all. When, and if, he was ready to talk, the rabbi would summon his words carefully, as if from a distance, marshaling them into his own strange semblance of order before presenting her with an explanation. He would begin slowly, like a medium speaking from a trance, his body stiff and his voice guttural, his words gradually gaining momentum until they tumbled over each other, the marvelous Rs rolling off his tongue like a verbal caress. But today it was different.

"Hurry, we haven't got all day here, and I need your help," he said, annoyed.

Only a few more steps down a slight decline and over a ridge, and there, at the edge of the immense boulder, perilously close to falling into the river, was the rabbi picking flowers!

Better not look down. Turning her gaze away from the murky water, Sharon knelt beside him. There must be a reason for this, she assured herself. He's never done anything like it before, so there has to be a very good reason for us to be in this place.

As if reading her thoughts, Rabbi Joachim turned to her and said, "Don't be afraid. The ground is safe here; I've been here before." Still, he did not extend his hand to steady her. "This is our next project," he said, pointing to a clump of purple clover neatly stuffed into his hat.

"But—"

"To look at it, you'd think it was nothing, just a simple herb growing in the crevices of these rocks," he said, glancing just past her as he spoke. "But, like all the wonderful secrets God has put before us here on Earth, it is so obvious as to be hidden from gross eyes."

"It looks like clover," said Sharon, relieved that he had returned to his familiar didacticism.

"Yes, nothing but a bunch of clover, a weed—but containing a great mystery." He sat down on the grass. Tired of kneeling, Sharon modestly tucked her dress under her knees and sat down across from him. A yellow butterfly fluttered past the rabbi's head.

"Sharon, this little plant is going to make a fortune for the Center. What would you say if I told you that it will cure mental illness, and even drug addiction?" he asked, his face glowing with excitement.

Knowing full well that the rabbi didn't really want an answer but was waiting for a sign of her unconditional faith in his judgment, Sharon nodded. What did she care about the alfalfa or clover or whatever it was that her dearest love was now holding out for her to admire? What she wanted was for the rabbi to graze her cheek playfully with the fuzzy tips of those purple flowers before tossing them aside, pushing her tenderly onto the soft wet grass and bringing his body down on hers, his hard, brightly colored pens pressing against her breasts.

But he was still speaking to her: "...when the idea first came to me. Strange, isn't it?"

I love you, my darling. Deafened by the voice inside her head, Sharon had missed the first part of the rabbi's sentence.

"I was driving on the West Side Highway when I first saw them— no, not once, but twice, first uptown and then downtown. They were standing in the island dividing the highway, two little Chinese ladies in blue aprons, bent over, actually, gathering what looked like ordinary weeds and putting them into a pair of wide straw baskets. At first I mistook them for sanitation people, you know, the ones who pick up highway litter with a pointed stick. But, no, they were two little Chinese women, just as I'd thought, gathering weeds along the West Side Highway."

Why don't you kiss me now? Why are you babbling about Chinese women and pointed sticks?

"Sharon, are you listening?"

"Rabbi Joachim, I—I'm sorry, I don't understand."

The rabbi frowned. "There's nothing to understand, Mrs. Berg. It's as simple as today's being Wednesday," he shrugged. Then, turning his back on the gross world she inhabited, he mused gently to himself: "I was reminded by the sight of them of something I had read in a work by the sixteenth-century Kabbalist Chayim Vital, a fragment that deals with curative herbs. And it suddenly struck me that the one herb he describes for curing addiction and other mental derangements is really nothing more than a form of clover!

"On my way to Monsey one afternoon, I stopped near here to think about it further. The image of those two Chinese women haunted me. I had to put together the pieces of this puzzle. Then, as always when I have been most deeply engaged in solving a problem, my master helped me. It was he who spoke to me, guiding me to this place.

'My son, why do you worry so about money for the Center when you are standing this very minute on a gold mine—and more importantly, on the very answer to one of man's worst afflictions?' As soon as the master had finished speaking to me, I started to search the grass—foolishly at first—looking for gold. After an hour of pointless searching the answer came to me—clearly, so clearly!"

Rabbi Joachim pulled a stalk of clover out of the ground and handed it to her. "Here it is, Sharon, our new project—CLOVER!"

THREE

IT HAD BEEN A DAY OF INADVERTENT FASTING so Sharon
was famished by the time Rabbi Joachim pulled up to Priceman's
Bookstore on Delancey Street and parked the car in front of a
tow-away zone notice. Except for having one tepid cup of coffee before
leaving the Center that morning, she had eaten nothing. But then,
neither had Rabbi Joachim, to whom it had never seemed to occur
that she, a less enlightened mortal, might be hungry. He'd probably
assumed that she, too, fed on the "manna" of the spirit, and that her
excitement about the new project had, like his own, obliterated most
of the baser necessities. The rabbi's single trip to the bathroom to wash
his hands before ritually blessing his Styrofoam cup of black coffee
would have been too short for him to pee. By contrast, as if proof of
her own spiritual shortcomings, Sharon's single cup had prompted
three trips to the toilet.

Attributing her now painful surge of hunger to the three greasy
non-Kosher frankfurters she noticed rotating on a spit in the window
of a neighboring diner, Sharon averted her eyes and followed Rabbi

Joachim into the bookstore with her stomach growling. Working six long, feverish days each week in a perennial race against printing deadlines while living on the rabbi's diet of coffee and an occasional hardboiled egg, she'd dropped ten pounds since starting her job at the Center, which, given the fact that she was tall, thin-legged, and narrow-hipped to begin with, made her as thin as a model. Before meeting Rabbi Joachim, Sharon wouldn't have thought twice about going into the diner and ordering a non-Kosher frank, but that was no longer possible. She'd barely worked for him a week when, to reinforce her observance of Jewish law, he'd come to her apartment, and after ritually "Koshering" the kitchen by reciting the *libun* purification blessing as he scalded the sink, stove, pots, pans, and cutlery with boiling water, he'd forbidden her to touch non-Kosher food from that day forward.

Throughout the ritual, Pinnie had watched the rabbi noncom-mittally. Though she'd never brought ham or bacon into the house and only ate Chinese food "on the outside" with her canasta friends after Sharon's Bubbe had died, Pinnie had, technically at least, kept a Kosher household, even if she had been fairly loose about mixing meat and milk dishes and silverware. But until recently, Sharon—led at first by her transgressing sister Arleen, and later by her nonobservant Jewish husband—hadn't bothered keeping Kosher at all. This made her wonder how her children, who were used to eating bacon and eggs for breakfast and pepperoni pizza for lunch, would react to the latest dietary changes. Falling back on packaged frankfurters stamped "Kosher" had been her temporary solution to the problem.

But now that she was thinking about food, Sharon found it odd that she'd never seen the rabbi eat anything but a hard-boiled egg or drink anything but black coffee. She'd once seen him *almost* eat a croissant at the home of a rich, widowed patron who'd pledged ten thousand dollars toward building a center affiliate in Los Angeles—

but that didn't count because he'd never actually taken a bite. The visit had been prompted by the widow's frantic telephone call one Sunday morning. Sharon had answered the phone and been bombarded by the hysterical woman's demand that Rabbi Joachim come to her home immediately and perform an exorcism. Claiming to be tormented by what she believed were "spirit noises," the widow, Mrs. Wolstein, said she believed that the spirits were malevolent because they always appeared as she was sitting down to meditate on the Holy Name—and since her two Persian cats had refused to emerge from their hiding place under the sofa for three days, she was convinced that the spirits were starving them to death.

Taking the telephone from Sharon, Rabbi Joachim had calmly informed Mrs. Wolstein that Jews were prohibited from dealing with spirits from the time of King Saul's visit to the Witch of Endor and recommended posting *mezuzahs* containing the Sacred Name of God over every door of her home. When his advice didn't calm Mrs. Wolstein sufficiently, the rabbi reluctantly agreed to go in person to see what he could do—taking Sharon along as a buffer against the widow's onslaught.

Dressed in a stunning purple silk suit dress, the bejeweled Mrs. Wolstein opened the door of her opulent Upper East Side townhouse herself and invited the rabbi in for tea. Sharon was swiftly rewarded for having accompanied her mentor by the familiar sound of his cough of disapproval. Following the widow, Sharon entered the library and sat down on the sofa, pretending to examine a book on wildflowers on the coffee table.

"Don't lose my place, dear," Mrs. Wolstein said, flashing a frigid smile.

Sharon turned a page, leaving a nasty fold directly across the page showing an illustration of the root of a wild sweet pea. Looking up from the book, she noted that the rabbi was standing in the opposite corner of the room with his back to Mrs. Wolstein, studying a Ben Shahn line drawing of a Hasidic Jew in a black beaver hat. From the tilt of his head, Sharon could tell that he'd left the everyday world and was mystically absorbed in the higher realms, and she relished the intimacy of his gesture. Except for his wife, she was the only woman who, if even for the briefest moments, knew him in a way she was sure Mrs. Wolstein—for all her money—never would.

As the widow ranted on about the spirits, Rabbi Joachim emerged from his meditative moment and reluctantly sat down on a silk butterfly chair that was too small for him. Just then a maid entered with three tea cups and a basket of croissants on a lacquered tray.

"Is this Kosher?" the rabbi asked. He reached into the basket and held up a croissant to inspect.

The maid patted the corners of her apron and stared at him.

"What?" shrieked the rabbi's visibly jolted patroness.

"I asked if this pastry is Kosher."

"Well, uh," Mrs. Wolstein stuttered, eyeing the smirking maid. "But of course, dear Rabbi Joachim, of course it's Kosher."

"Are you sure it isn't baked with lard?"

The maid shuffled her weight from one leg to the next.

"Stop that fidgeting, Mary," Mrs. Wolstein snapped. "Why, no, it's pure butter, I think...." She trailed off.

Sharon tried looking away, but Mrs. Wolstein had caught her eye and gave her another frigid smile.

"Butter, that's all right if it's not combined with meat. Do any of these pastries contain meat?"

The maid shook her head.

"Okay, then, which way is the bathroom?" asked the rabbi, getting up to wash his hands.

Mrs. Wolstein had the maid show him to the front hall bathroom.

Sharon was wondering why people were always calling toilets 'bathrooms,' 'lavatories,' 'rest rooms,' and 'powder rooms' instead of just plain 'toilets' when Mrs. Wolstein, taking advantage of the rabbi's absence, turned to her and pleaded, "What shall I do, Mrs. Berg? I certainly don't know whether these croissants are Kosher or not."

Shrugging her shoulders, Sharon returned the widow's frigid smile.

"Oh!" On the verge of tears, Mrs. Wolstein slapped at the sofa under which, Sharon presumed, the starving Persian cats were lurking. "Mary! What are you standing there for, go get the tea!" the widow screamed, causing the maid to flee to the kitchen.

Rabbi Joachim returned, and was about to take a bite out of his croissant when the room was suddenly filled with the muffled sound of an explosion and the smell of burning rubber. The maid bolted into the living room, wringing her hands.

"The teapot's burst—the water boiled out and the teapot's burst. Even the Pyrex, madam, and there's melted plastic everywhere!"

"So it's *not* Kosher, just as I expected," Rabbi Joachim announced jubilantly, and tossed the croissant back on the plate. "That was the sign. What made you think you could get away with such a lie?"

"But, Rabbi," Mrs. Wolstein pleaded to no effect, for Rabbi Joachim had put his hat on over his yarmulke and was already beckoning Sharon to follow him to the front door.

"You can eat what you like, Mrs. Wolstein, but you should know better than to serve non-Kosher cakes to an Orthodox rabbi," he admonished the desperate woman, who was now clinging to his coat sleeve.

"Wait, don't go! Please! I'll send out for some Kosher food," the widow cried, blocking his exit. Rabbi Joachim did not move; religious conviction prohibited him from prying her fingers from his person.

Mrs. Wolstein then opted for a more dignified approach to her situation. In a milk-curdling voice, she said, "Very well, my dear Rabbi Joachim, about that ten-thousand-dollar pledge of mine—you can just forget it." Loosening her grip on his sleeve, she shook her wrists and jangled her bracelets for emphasis.

"Suit yourself," said Rabbi Joachim, stepping out into the street with Sharon following close behind him. "We don't need bribes, thank you."

"Goodbye, and don't bother calling me if you change your mind and decide to apologize tomorrow," Mrs. Wolstein screamed. "As far as I'm concerned, we're finished!" She walked back into the house, slamming the door behind her.

The widow stood by her promise, for the money, due to be transferred into the Center's account that very week, never arrived. But that wasn't all. Vowing to destroy him, she would use her insider's knowledge of the proposed "clover cure," and her powerful social and political connections, in honing her revenge against the Rabbi.

FOUR

HENRY NOVALIS, A CITY COLLEGE ENGINEERING graduate student and recent Hare Krishna defector to the Center for Mystical Judaism, had introduced Rabbi Joachim to Seymour Priceman, the Center's publisher and distributor. While complaining to anyone who would listen of declining sales, the cost of keeping up with the new technologies, and threatening to close his bookstore for good, Seymour had managed nevertheless to expand what had once been his father's hole-in-the-wall "magic shop" into a two-storey gold mine of the occult. From his profits, he'd contracted with a Varick Street printer to publish out-of-print theosophical books, a "sideline" that had caught on so well as to bypass his enormously successful bookstore trade. It did not take long before several big uptown publishers were offering to buy him out, yet despite his eighty-hour week and increasingly troublesome varicose veins, Seymour refused to sell.

Professing never to have read even one of the thousands of books lining the store's shelves, Seymour enjoyed putting off newcomers with his apparent indifference to anything but hard cash. And to the casual browser, he certainly must have appeared out of place among the ornate Indian incense trays, Tibetan mandalas, and Chinese acupuncture posters cramming his bookstore. But among his intimates, Seymour Priceman was known as a true believer, ready to extend a helping hand to the yogis, astrologers, water-diviners, vegans, and witches who'd cultivated his friendship over the years.

In addition to his father's magic shop, Seymour had also inherited the old man's mild-mannered disposition. Nothing seemed to rattle him, not even the ill-tempered crew who worked for, and in the case of his relatives, against him, or Wanda, the sweet but absent-minded medium who erratically maintained his correspondence. In the course of a year, Sharon had gotten to know them all, the ubiquitous Priceman nephews, the sons and daughters-in-law—the whole sullen lot of them. And as she'd gotten to know them better, they began confiding in her their schemes for building condominiums in Las Vegas, their worries over the increasing not-so-petty thefts of expensive first editions, and their frustrations over Seymour's maddening nonchalance in the face of those thefts. She had been insulted only once, by her least favorite Priceman relative, Seymour's bald uncle, Morris, who had called Rabbi Joachim a "con artist" and Sharon "the rabbi's bimbo" to her face. But that hadn't stopped her from loving the store with its thousands of tightly crammed volumes on shelves circled by steel tracks and mobile ladders, sale tables overflowing with a mixture of dusty treasure and junk, and best of all, the disembodied mannequin hand with beringed fingers pointing to way to the Occult Specialty and Personal Service Department downstairs. There, in a cavernous basement dominated by an ancient green sofa flanked by equally ancient chrome tables, she would poke around in the books, walking among the Haitian priestesses, turbaned Indian yogis, and garishly rouged psychics who frequented the place while Rabbi Joachim privately "talked business" with his publisher.

Late in the afternoon on the day of their Palisades adventure, as the rabbi sat in Seymour's office describing the long-range benefits of clover on the ills of mankind, Sharon came across an earlier edition of Mrs. Wolstein's book on wildflowers among a pile of discards in the Occult Specialty and Personal Service Department. Its cover was shredded and its title page had been marked by a shoe heel. Wondering if there were some significant connection between the unfortunate day at the widow's townhouse and her coming upon the same book now, Sharon turned to the index, found the entry on "Clover," and sat down to read.

> *Rabbit-foot, Old Field, or Stone Clover Trifolium arvense Linnaeus. An erect, usually much-branched annual, 5 to 18 inches high, silky-pubescent. Leaves very short petioled, three-foliate, oblanceolate or linear, minutely toothed, blunt and sometimes notched at the apex, narrowed at the base, one-half to 1 inch long. Flowers sessile in dense, terminal peduncled, oblong or cylindric heads, one-half to 1 inch long; calyx very silky; corolla whitish, shorter than the elongated, slender, plumose calyx lobes. Fruiting pod very small.*
>
> *In waste places, dry and sandy fields, roadsides, etc. Quebec and Ontario to South Carolina, Florida, Tennessee and Missouri. Naturalized from Europe. Flowering from May to September...*

There seemed to be nothing special about the plant, and there was no mention at all of its curative properties. The author evidently had felt that clover didn't even warrant a photograph. Sharon turned the page and immersed herself in the entry on foxgloves, which included a glossy color plate. How nakedly sexual, these plants, she thought.

Here was one that resembled a man's penis, and there, another, a violet-colored flower with the soft, undulating mound of a woman's vulva—

Someone was motioning to her.

It was one of the new clerks, an angry, stringy-haired girl wearing thick glasses. "Please put that book down," she said in a sharp, nasal voice. "That group is not for sale."

A gnome-sized man who had been reading avidly at Sharon's side commiserated with her in a whisper. "They're tough here, aren't they?" He winked, giving her a buck-toothed grin. "I'd go somewhere else, but they got the best selection in the city."

Sharon smiled and nodded politely. Not wanting to open a conversation with the man while at the same trying to avoid the familiar sneer of Seymour's Uncle Morris, she sat down on the sofa and was rescued by the white-haired medium's offer of a cup of coffee.

Seeing Rabbi Joachim emerge from the glass-enclosed office with Seymour behind him, Sharon knew immediately that it had been a hard battle, but that the rabbi had managed to enlist his backing on the clover project. Seymour's surly Uncle Morris had also been watching. Seeing the triumphant look on his enemy's face, he slunk away to eavesdrop on the two men from behind the bookshelves.

"One more stop, Mrs. Berg, then I'll drive you home," Rabbi Joachim said, hurrying her up the stairs. Reaching the top step, he turned and called over his shoulder to Seymour, "I'll talk to you more about the trip over the telephone, Priceman. And remember, your *full* participation, no matter what happens!"

Minutes later, Sharon found herself on the Bowery, waiting in the car in front of a basement herbalist's shop while the rabbi deliberated with the owner among barrels of Korean ginseng root. Judging from his determined stride as he emerged from the shop, she knew he'd been unsuccessful at getting the herbalist's endorsement for the clover cure but remained undaunted. It wasn't until ten o'clock that night when, after driving around the city for hours, Rabbi Joachim finally located an herbalist working out of an apartment near the Bronx Zoo who was willing to work with him on the clover project.

When he pulled up in front of Sharon's house at eleven-thirty, the rabbi did not get out of the car to open the door for her. Nor, after pushing up his hat and revealing the furrow mark on his forehead—a mark as startling as a flower stalk, as distinctive as a clover leaf, which, as the book had told her, grew only in barren wasted places—did Rabbi Joachim wish her good night. He simply leaned out the window and called to her as an afterthought, "By the way, Mrs. Berg, I'll be leaving for about three weeks—to Israel and then on to London. There's some research I must do myself—some basic groundwork to cover before we start to try this thing out. Take care of the office while I'm gone, will you? Come to think of it, you don't have to go in every day. Rabbi Tayson's Zohar classes don't start again until September. Turn on the answering machine. At the latest, I should be back by the end of August. I'll call you."

Dazed by the rabbi's sudden, offhanded announcement of his departure, Sharon stumbled toward the house. Halfway up the walk to the porch, she heard him add, "Take some time off for yourself. You could use the rest." Then he drove away, turning the corner at top speed with the tires screeching.

Now her head was throbbing as she felt the first tentacles of a migraine coming on. By the time she got to the door, she could barely see well enough to get her key in the lock. Once inside, on the foyer table, she found a partly effaced note on her daughter's Magic Slate board.

There are some chicken breasts in the fridge when, and if, you get home tonight. You had two phone calls—one from Barney the pig, and the other from Rabbi Tayson. He doesn't want Paulie in the day camp anymore, and he wants to see you about the fall term. Phyllis had a temperature today—100—so I didn't let her go into the pool. Her nose is running also, I thought you might like to know. Don't wake me when you go to bed tonight, my day was hell.

—Pinnie

P.S. The mailman brought this letter to the door today. He says it got to the wrong address first. I gave him a dollar tip.

Sharon was now so nauseated she could barely tolerate the lingering smell of the fried chicken breasts Pinnie had prepared for her, no less eat them. Still reeling from the Rabbi's casual brushoff, and too distracted to fully absorb her mother's bad news, she would have to delay dealing with the children's problems until she'd recovered sufficiently herself. And not only from the migraine. It would be a long, painful night. She turned up the fringed table cover she'd tried sewing to calm her nerves during her dragged-out divorce proceedings. It was full of holes and looked more like a rag than a table cover. A blot of clay had been rubbed indelibly into center of the cloth. The letter she found underneath it invited her to bring her grievance against one Jorge Diaz of 171 East 118th Street, New York, NY to Room 104B of the Criminal Courts Building on Centre Street that Friday.

FIVE

HAT DID SHARON KNOW OF COURTROOMS?
One divorce and a reading of her father's will com-
prised her entire contact with the law. On the subway,
between the Nevins Street and Borough Hall stops, she thought of
getting off the train and skipping court. Nobody would miss her, there
were a thousand Jorge Diaz cases being dismissed due to "no-show"
complainants today. Hadn't the arresting policeman told her that
himself? What would one less matter? But now it was too late; the
train had already pulled into the Chambers Street station. As usual,
her indecisiveness had cost her. Something apart from all her doubts
and reasons for turning back had urged her on—a bracketed bit of
curiosity, a wish to see whether any of the characters in her Coney
Island drama would in fact appear. Would Jorge Diaz, for instance,
be wearing his beanie? Had Officer Edward Pols been transferred to
another precinct for accepting bribes from the numbers men along
his beat? Was the girlfriend of her rescuer, Junior Cantana, delivering
a baby on this very Friday? Did Junior Cantana even have a girlfriend?

She didn't remember his saying anything about a girlfriend or a wife when presenting himself as a witness to the attempted robbery. What if she were the only one to show up? In that case, she would have to salvage the day somehow, maybe take the subway uptown to the New York Public Library's Forty-Second Street branch and gather lists of ancient references to herbal cures in preparation for Rabbi Joachim's return.

Outside the open door of the courtroom a knot of policemen, caps in hand, had gathered around a drinking fountain in the niche of a wall, where an unbroken flow of water dribbled halfway up before turning back again into the drain. Every so often one of them would bend over and slurp up a mouthful of water before rejoining his comrades. They were an uncongenial crew, patting the guns in their open holsters and fanning themselves with their caps. One was pockmarked and another had the same narrow mean eyes of the defendant she expected to face in the courtroom. Not one of them moved aside to let her through.

Room 104B was air-conditioned, but insufficiently, and in the only open seat in the last row, which Sharon immediately took, it was stifling. The benches were crowded with overheated human flesh, much of it unwashed. The judge had not yet arrived. Various clerks and nervous young assistant D.A.s were flitting back and forth like moths in front of the empty bench; the court stenographer was already stationed at her post; and the security guards were standing at attention in their sweat-stained shirts. One of them, an elderly man with a bulbous red nose, stood meditating on a predetermined spot on the wall. Something in his manner, the way he'd cut himself off from the mundane proceedings around him, made Sharon think of Rabbi Joachim. But of course the comparison was ridiculous; the two men had nothing in common at all. The guard wasn't meditating, he was probably trying to fend off a hangover from last night's drinking binge. As for Rabbi

Joachim, what, except for the story about his Kabbalist uncle, did she really know of his life beyond the office? Nothing. All she could say for certain was that on the very Friday she was seated on a bench in Room 104B between a black woman in a platinum blond wig wearing the tiniest, tightest pair of orange shorts, and a pink-faced young man with a sleeping baby in his lap, Rabbi Joachim, was aloft, on his way to his wife in Israel. Her next thought brought the blood rushing to her face: the Orthodox Jewish injunction commanding a man to *lie with his wife* on the evening of his return from a journey.

Rabbi Joachim's absence gnawed like a rat at her heart.

Taking a tissue from her purse, Sharon dabbed at the beads of perspiration that had gathered above her lip then fanned her face, giving it up when the effort only made her hotter. Several people around her were talking to each other in Spanish. A snaggle-toothed woman in a red satin blouse with a gold crucifix dangling over her immense protruding bosom seemed to be complaining bitterly. Sharon wondered if the woman was related to Jorge Diaz. Could it be his mother? His sister? His girlfriend? How many Diazes were surrounding her, flashing their crucifixes on exposed bosoms? Overwhelmed by the heat of her neighbors' bodies, Sharon felt herself on the verge of another migraine.

The judge was now, unconscionably, ten minutes late. She glanced around the courtroom but found no sign of her Coney Island cast of characters. The sleeping baby in the arms of the man next to her woke up and started to cry. The man didn't make a move to calm the baby but sat looking fixedly ahead at the empty judge's bench.

"Mrs. Berg?" Someone in the aisle was trying to get her attention. Sharon looked up and instantly recognized the five-o-clock-shadowed face of Officer Pols.

"Oh, where are you sitting? I didn't see you when I came in."

"We've been here for thirty minutes, waiting for you."

The woman in the tight shorts either could not, or would not, move, forcing Sharon to climb over her and step on the toe of the pink-faced man with the crying baby.

"We?" she asked, following Officer Pols to the second row, closer to the window housing the poorly functioning air-conditioner, where it was only slightly cooler. What did one call him: "Officer," "Mr. Pols," "Ed?" Probably best not to call him anything.

"Yeah, Mr. Cantana and myself. We've been waiting for you, looking around all over the place," he said, hurrying ahead. "Hey, I found her, here she is," he shouted into the second row from the aisle.

"Hello there, still have your pocketbook, I see," Junior Cantana said, his movie-star face illuminated with his perfect smile. He looked out of place sitting there in court, like an unexpected ray of color in a black-and-white photograph. All traces of the "army grunt" wrestling with Jorge Diaz on the beach at Coney Island were gone. She had judged Mr. Cantana too quickly the first time. Was her irrational attachment to her charismatic and unreachable Kabbalah master at fault? Or, more likely, could her frustrated love for Rabbi Joachim, her fantasied savior, be turning her into a man-hater? She'd read somewhere that it often happened to single women, as they got older. No, Sharon thought irritably as she crammed into a seat on the bench next to him, it's just that the guy is wearing a suit and you can't see that tacky skull pendant around his neck. Nonetheless, when Junior Cantana politely moved away and surrendered most of his seat to her, Sharon could not help noticing that he smelled pleasantly of trees in the rain.

An increasingly anxious Officer Pols was desperately trying to engage her in a conversation about the weather. Having exhausted that subject and gotten little response, he launched an attack on the city's prison system by cataloguing the horrors he'd personally seen while on duty at the Tombs. A graphic portrayal of a prison riot was followed by an analysis of its causes. Ten more minutes passed, and still no judge. Sharon complimented Officer Pols for his open-mindedness, which prompted a further discussion of the inefficiencies of the justice system.

Junior Cantana, she noticed, was staring at her.

The snaggle-toothed woman in the red satin blouse had gotten up from her seat and approached the court stenographer demanding to know where the judge was. The court stenographer alerted the two security guards, who ushered the woman back to her seat.

Junior Cantana wondered aloud why the judge was so late, causing Officer Pols to launch yet another catalogue of complaints against the system of "revolving door justice" characterized by one-hundred and fifty working days, five hours, three hundred minutes and an infinite number of seconds spent by the average police officer sitting in court, waiting for judges who invariably arrived late only to suspend sentences anyway.

Sharon yawned. Something opened and closed deep inside her gut—the result of breakfasting on two hurried cups of black coffee. She needed to go to the toilet.

"I hope Jorge Diaz shows up," said Junior Cantana.

"Don't be surprised if he doesn't," Officer Pols shrugged.

Just then the judge arrived.

Case after case droned on, an endless litany of petty crimes, felonies, prostitution, pimping. Witnesses appeared, and so did plaintiffs—five of them bandaged. A constant stream of "no-shows" and suspended sentences elicited sarcastic quips from the judge. When the husband of the woman in the red satin blouse was finally led to the docket, she stood up and called to him sharply in Spanish. Again, the guards forced her to sit down. The husband, a small man with a pencil mustache and drug-befuddled eyes, bowed his head at the laughter of the court.

Sharon went to the toilet and returned. People were clustered around the doorways of every hearing room along the corridor. Out of one there emerged the loud soundtrack of what an onlooker informed her was an allegedly pornographic film. According to Sharon's informant, it was a private hearing and the door should have been closed, but the air-conditioner had broken down and the judge had ordered it be opened. Sharon looked into the courtroom and saw that the shades were drawn. In the ribbon of light coming from the film projector, through dancing motes of dust, she saw that the room was packed with men. A microsecond's glance at the screen in front revealed a naked man mounting a naked woman from behind. Sharon walked away, but still heard the sound of exaggerated moaning as the actors climaxed.

There had been no toilet paper in the stall so she'd been forced to use the crumpled tissues in her purse. The hot water faucets had run only cold water. For the past two days she'd been suffering from premenstrual cramps. On her way back to Room 104B, she'd been propositioned by a pimp in a pink fedora. Down the hall another pimp was berating a woman standing in front of him staring down at her platform wedges, calling her "a good-for-nothing flat-tit bitch!"

"Don't bother trying to get through," said Officer Pols as Sharon prepared to make her way back to her seat. "It's a no-show. They've got a bench warrant out for him. Stay put. I'll go up and talk to the D.A.'s man and see if I can get you another date quick."

She wanted to tell him not to bother, that she wasn't coming back to this place, not ever, but Officer Pols had already gotten up and was approaching the bench. The judge had just called a recess and people were milling around everywhere. A woman was sobbing bitterly in a corner behind the American flag. Two lawyers hurried past her joking about the "allegedly" pornographic film screening next door.

"Well, I guess that's that," Junior Cantana said, sticking his hands into his jacket pockets.

"This is ridiculous," Sharon said, "I don't even know what I'm doing here in the first place." What would Rabbi Joachim think of her standing in the aisle of a packed courtroom shoulder to shoulder with this goy?

"Same as me, doing your duty as a citizen," Junior said.

"But you came all the way from Pennsylvania, for me it was only a subway ride."

"I've traveled much further than that, for a *cause*," he retorted. Why that mocking tone? Did he really mean for her to take him seriously?

Announcing the adjournment of hearings until two o'clock, the bailiff ordered everyone out of the courtroom, and Sharon and Junior inched their way out of the crowded aisle. They had lost sight of Officer Pols, who could now be seen elbowing a path through the milling crowd in the corridor. "Good news!" he called, waving. "Meet me outside."

In the crowded lobby, frustrated plaintiffs were cursing the system in a variety of languages, the families of those who'd been convicted were condemning the judge to hell, and a bondsman standing next to a trash basket was contemptuously spitting on the floor. A security guard saw him but shrugged his shoulders and went outside for a smoke.

"Listen, I talked to the judge himself—he knows me from being here so often—and he absolutely assured me that they'd have your character here on the nineteenth. How's that?" Officer Pols asked as Sharon approached him in front of the courthouse.

"Look, you're awfully kind to go through so much inconvenience for me, but..."

What was all this excitement over one more junkie? It wasn't as if Jorge Diaz had actually gotten away with her purse. He hadn't really laid a hand on her, so it couldn't be called an assault case, and the purse had been retrieved intact.

"So you'll meet me here on the nineteenth at nine-thirty on the dot?"

"I don't know."

Officer Pols' face clouded over with disappointment.

"Why does it matter so much to you?" Sharon finally gathered the courage to ask.

Officer Pols started to answer, but a fight had broken out at the entrance and she couldn't hear him over the hooting and booing of the crowd. Junior Cantana was pushed up against her as the opponents were quickly pulled apart and led away by two policemen. Sharon blushed, hurriedly excused herself, pulled away and turned again to Officer Pols.

"I have a job. I don't think I'll be able to make it."

"Mrs. Berg, how are we going to get these operators off the streets if people like you aren't going to help?"

"But why me?" she pleaded, pointing to different people in the crowd. "Look here, look over there, look at all these people!"

"Yeah, look at them, and then take a good look at yourself. See any difference?" Pointing at her and then at Junior Cantana, Officer Pols said heatedly, "It's gotta be people like you and him who can speak up. That's who the judges and the smart-guy D.A.s'll listen to—not them."

"It's obviously very important to the man," said Junior Cantana.

"Yeah, I'll say it's important. I got a kid in high school, a sixteen-year-old boy—on methadone," Officer Pols finished grimly.

"Oh," Sharon thought of her own problem son.

"You'll come, won't you?"

"And Mr. Cantana?" Sharon found herself asking aloud, for despite her reluctance, in fact lurking just below it, was the hope that

Junior Cantana would indeed be there to protect her, though from what, she didn't know.

"Be glad to," Junior offered.

"You sure it won't be inconvenient for you?"

"I can get away whenever I like. I'm a wounded war hero, remember."

Sharon again detected sarcasm in his voice.

Officer Pols shook Junior's hand. "Thanks, thanks. I'll be looking out for both of you on the nineteenth, then. Same time, same place. Don't disappoint me, now," he said, pointing his finger at Sharon before melting back into the crowd.

SIX

"**I**SN'T IT UNHEALTHY to let yourself get so skinny?"
Junior asked bluntly.

"According to the latest research, rats on a starvation
diet live twice as long as those on a normal daily calorie intake."

"But you're not a rat."

They were "Junior" and "Sharon" now, seated across from each
other in the red vinyl booth of a luncheonette on the ground floor of a
bondsman's office building, sipping the froth from their cappuccinos.

He'd maneuvered her through the densely packed courthouse
corridors, carving a path through chattering lawyers and their laconic
clients just wide enough for her to walk in, down the crowded grand
marble staircase all the way to the front door. When three women
lawyers near the newspaper stand in the lobby interrupted their
conversation to stare at her handsome escort, Sharon had permitted
herself to smile at them for envying her.

Officer Pols had left them standing together on the courthouse
steps beset by a sudden dank wind that drove noisily past them under

a storm-lid of darkness. Discarded newspapers thrashed against the curbstones, were temporarily airborne and then roughly deposited into running streams of water from the sewers at opposite ends of the street. Store gratings jiggled madly in their sockets; a flock of pigeons huddling under a tree for safety fought among themselves for a few shriveled grains of dried corn, remnants of the local "bird lady's" early morning scatterings. Gathering their sparse harvest in their beaks, the greedy pigeons churned their wings and dispersed. The dark wind screamed and howled, vacuuming leaves from the trees and spewing a bolus of black dust into the mouth of the subway on the corner.

Junior had shielded her from the wind as, without having formally agreed to, they walked together toward the BMT. When they were halfway down the block, lightning sliced through the swollen clouds and it started pouring. "Let's make a run for it," he shouted over the noise of the wind, pointing at the restaurant across the street.

Hardy's Luncheonette was filled with construction workers from a nearby site; idled by the storm, they had taken up every seat at the counter. One of them, a boy wearing a t-shirt with cutoff sleeves, looked too young to be a construction worker. He reminded Sharon of the Coney Island teenager who had operated the Whip when she was a kid, and then of the whole chain of events that had resulted in her sitting in the booth of a non-Kosher restaurant having lunch with a "stranger"—which, as Rabbi Joachim had informed her, was the literal meaning of the Hebrew word "goy." As if to compound her transgression, the menu consisted entirely of meat dishes of the "ham steak" variety, and she refused to order anything to eat until Junior finally convinced the waitress to bring them meatless Swiss cheese sandwiches.

The construction workers were drinking beer and talking loudly, but instead of being annoyed, Sharon found their boisterous conversation a comforting diversion from her growing interest in Junior

Cantana. She could hardly keep from staring at his sensuous lips and wondering what they would feel like pressing on her mouth. Her neck. Her breasts. No, no, that wouldn't do. Could it be that her glimpsing the pornographic film in the tumid erotic atmosphere of that man-filled courtroom was belatedly exercising its effect on her? Or the fact that her period was coming on, redolent with the forbidden sexual overtones of Jewish orthodoxy? Quickly, she turned her glance back to the construction workers. When they could no longer hold her attention, she was assailed by the image of Rabbi Joachim, his resplendent voice fading to a whisper as he described the Kabbalistic miracles and wonders performed by his late uncle. Filled with dread and highly stressed at the sudden onset of well-hidden unfulfilled sexual longings bedeviling her since her divorce, Sharon felt a familiar tightness in her scalp—the hovering, ever-present threat of a migraine. This was accompanied by a flush of shame as she relived the near orgasmic experience of watching the rabbi enter the higher realms before leaving her behind with this Italian, this *goy*, sitting across from her in this duct-taped booth, offering lunch and a summer rainstorm's-worth of male company. And what was she offering in return: a mournful expression and the refusal to order anything but coffee until he'd coaxed her into letting him order the cheese sandwiches? Sharon pulled two paper napkins from their holder, tore one in the process, and handed the whole one to Junior.

Marble-sized raindrops furiously pelted the windows. In the booth behind her, a man cursed the weather. A construction worker at the counter picked his teeth with the edge of a book of matches.

"Ain't you got no color TV in this place?" he complained to the counterman.

"Sure, that's all we're missing around here," mumbled the droopy-eyed counterman, waving an armful of colorful tattoos.

Sharon took another ramble through the punitive wood of Jewish guilt. Hadn't she just been over this ground?

"So, why 'Junior,' why not—well, what is your real name? I've forgotten it," she said in an effort to break the absent Rabbi Joachim's stranglehold. Unnerved by her sexual longings, and without wanting to, she'd gone on the offensive, adopting a carping tone to mask her ambivalence about her attraction to the handsome goy who'd sat silently watching her.

"Carlo, my real name is Carlo. But nobody ever calls me that. It's my father's name, too. We used to get mixed up all the time, so my mother started calling me Junior and I kind of got used to it," he said, almost apologetically. Clearly, she wasn't the only one who felt uncomfortable.

"Junior," Sharon murmured. It was an alien name.

Since neither of them seemed willing to discuss the attempted purse snatching that had brought them together in the first place, they lapsed into awkward silence. At the same time, both seemed to be lingering, deliberately dragging out their time together even as the downpour was stopping. Mercifully, their Swiss cheese sandwiches arrived then, and Junior resumed the conversation.

"You aren't on a diet, are you?"

"No."

"*You* certainly don't need to diet." Surprised at the vehemence of his own remark, he stopped abruptly.

He's getting even for my mocking his name, Sharon thought as she lifted the sandwich from the plate and began eating. "I usually work so hard that I forget to eat," she said.

"That's not good."

"I've inherited my father's genes for high cholesterol so I have to watch what I eat anyway."

"Okay. Peace." Holding up two fingers in a V, Junior smiled at her.

Glancing into the mirror over the counter, Sharon saw herself reflected as a mousy, blond older woman enjoying the flattery of a very handsome younger man. It suddenly dawned on her that Junior might have been teasing her, giving her the compliment—or the lie—of being a woman he found attractive, and therefore worthy of his concern for her health. Then again, maybe he wasn't teasing or lying. Maybe he really *was* attracted to her. She hadn't been out on a date for so long that she couldn't tell the difference. Rabbi Joachim's indifference to her physical presence didn't help, either. Consistent with her diminishing sense of self, her feeling of unworthiness, and her shame at being unloved and unlovable, Sharon's negative assessment of her looks somehow made her feel more "spiritual." Now Junior was calling that spiritual image into question, making her uncomfortable. Her face reddening, she bent over her plate so as not to see herself in the mirror. When she'd finished every crumb of her sandwich and devoured the pickle, Junior asked if she wanted more to eat.

"No thanks," Sharon said, wiping her mouth with the torn napkin. "I'd better get going, it's stopped raining," she said, the sour acid of penitence already rising in her stomach. She'd betrayed the rabbi, forfeiting the right to savor the forbidden food.

Junior paid the bill, wouldn't hear of her offering to contribute so much as the tip.

Outside, the rain had washed the streets clean, a pale sun was casting a beginning-of-the-world glow over the wet shop fronts, and people were tentatively emerging from their shelters. In the narrow, crooked Chinatown lane bordering the courthouse, a boy on a delivery bicycle piled high with greens half-stood in the saddle, whistling as he pedaled past them. On Canal Street, a man flipped a green tarpaulin from the stands flanking his hardware shop, disclosing piles of copper hobnails, chromium ball bearings, and iron rings whose shapes, Junior said, reminded him of modern sculpture.

Recalling their first meeting, Sharon asked, "Are you really an artist?"

She had barely gotten out the words when a horse leading a junk wagon, a cowbell ringing from its neck, stepped into an enormous puddle at a smart clip and drenched them both. Junior's light beige suit now had dark amoeba-shaped blotches at the knees and shins; Sharon's stockings were soaked and the hem of her dress was instantly dyed a cyanotic blue. They looked at each other and burst out laughing.

"Modern art!" Sharon giggled, pointing to Junior's ruined pants.

"Watercolors!" he called back between fits of laughter, pointing to her dress.

"W-what d-do *you* care? You've pr-probably gotten more s-suits like th-that one! This is my one g-good summer d-dress!" she shouted, her laughter mounting. It was crazy to be breaking down like this in the middle of the street, but she couldn't control herself.

"My *only* suit, you mean," he responded before giving way to a wild swell of laughter.

As soon as their laughter had subsided, it seemed perfectly natural that they spend the rest of the afternoon together. Junior suggested she might like to see an exhibit of political cartoons by Hogarth at the Pierpont Morgan Library, and Sharon, reminded of her father's thumb-smudged copy of *The Rake's Progress*, enthusiastically agreed.

How long had it been since she'd been with a man who really cared about paintings and books? Not since her father died—ending their weekly trips to the Brooklyn Museum, the ivy-covered library, the hours of avidly reading Dickens aloud together in the living room while Pinnie clattered about in the kitchen and Arleen painted watercolor family portraits in her bedroom. These days, even if Sharon had wanted to read for pleasure, she couldn't; it was hard enough trying to decipher the texts Rabbi Joachim had assigned her. She'd once gotten up the courage to complain of this to him, but the rabbi had waved her off, saying, "Only books like the Zohar have the power to open the psychic channels in the mind necessary for advanced meditation." Yet, no matter how long and hard she pondered the Zohar, no psychic channels opened in her mind—at least none that she was aware of. Rabbi Joachim had enigmatically responded to her failure by advising her to meditate more deeply on the mystery of Jewish suffering. Taking his advice, she'd spent the last few months meditating on the sections in Exodus describing the Egyptian enslavement of the children of Israel—still to no effect. Amazingly, it was not until today, standing next to Junior Cantana facing Hogarth's secular illustrations of daily human suffering, that she finally understood what Rabbi Joachim had meant.

"You really like this?" she asked, pointing into a glass case at a sketch of a vomiting drunkard.

"As a subject, do you mean?"

"Yes, the subject."

"Well, it's not the *Mona Lisa*, but it does just what the artist intended it to—it moves you, right?"

Grimacing, Sharon nodded.

"And the craftsmanship is unbeatable. Look at that hand, how alive it is. You can almost see the blood running through the veins. Do you know how long it takes to learn just to draw a *hand*," Junior pointed to a harlot in a lace cap holding hands with a paunchy customer.

"No, I can't draw. My sister supposedly can, but I haven't seen any of her work since she left home."

"Well, I started formal art lessons when I was at college. That seems like ages ago and, do you know, it still isn't easy. Hands are just not my thing, I guess. But noses, you should see my noses," Junior chuckled as he circled a glass case.

"Is that what you do for a living, draw?" Aware that she was stepping over the border of the purely sociable, Sharon wanted to know more about Junior Cantana; his vulnerability demanded it of her.

"That, and recuperate."

Sharon watched as he moved from sketch to sketch, now peering up close to the glass, now gazing from a distance, and now stopping to remove a pair of glasses from his breast pocket, putting them on and then taking them off again before replacing them in his pocket. Looking at the world, nose to nose with it—no wonder he was good at drawing noses. She liked the ease with which he moved and the way he had of being playful and earnest at the same time, his gestures assuring her that she could trust him. And while fearful of their mutual sexual attraction, she'd have liked to have him as a friend. Someone to remind her of her lost childhood, where, as trapper in coonskin, Indian, explorer, and detective, she and her father had roamed and conquered. Sharon briefly thought of telling him this, but held back. Their intimacy was still raw and tenuous, and, too, the fact that he was probably Catholic.

The morning's rain had come and gone like a vivid dream and the streets were now baking in the glare of a newly revived afternoon sun. It had become a scorching day. Walking alongside Junior Cantana, surrounded by office workers, dog walkers, and fashionable shoppers, immersed in the material world of the "shattered vessels" Rabbi Joachim had been training her to resist, Sharon was relieved when they reached Forty-Second Street.

"I can catch the subway here," she said.

Junior nodded. "See you on the nineteenth."

"Yes, see you then," she called as she entered the subway and descended the stairs without looking back, knowing that he'd remain standing there, watching her until she disappeared from view.

SEVEN

PAULIE HAD NEVER BEEN AN EASY CHILD to deal with. But after Sharon's divorce, his angry eruptions at home and at school had grown more frequent. When she could no longer dismiss his flare-ups as a "passing phase," she'd briefly consulted Rabbi Joachim—and gotten the enigmatic reply, "Change of place, change of luck," which she interpreted as a directive to take Paulie out of public school and enroll him at the Center for Mystical Judaism's Orthodox *Yeshiva Rav Shimon bar Yohai for Boys*. To make up for the inconvenient distance between her home in Flatbush and the yeshiva's location in Crown Heights, not to mention having to pay for a private school, Rabbi Joachim had arranged with his deputy, Rabbi Tayson, the yeshiva's principal, to give her a tuition waiver that included admission for Paulie to the summer day camp. Sharon had resisted at first, but gave in at the offer of the tuition waiver. Nonetheless, the transfer hadn't changed Paulie's behavior, which was the reason she now found herself traveling two hours by bus to get from Westminster Road to Eastern Parkway, with plenty of time to dread having to plead with

Rabbi Tayson to keep Paulie on. But what choice did she have when her son's conduct had deteriorated to the point where no other day camp would have him?

She and Pinnie had argued, and she'd left the house forgetting her wallet, with only enough change for round trip bus fare in her purse. Last night's conversation with Barney hadn't helped, either. When she'd called him, a woman had answered.

"Is Barney Berg there?"

"Barney—I think it's your ex-wife," the woman yelled into the mouth of the receiver without bothering to cover it. Sharon heard the magnified sound of her chewing gum, followed by the popping of a bubble.

Barney took the telephone, "Yeah?"

Picturing his pink, bald dome, Sharon asked, "Who was that?"

"Who?"

"That woman who answered."

"Oh, that was Irma, I'm going to marry her this coming winter."

"Congratulations."

A tense, long pause, then, finally, from Barney's end: "What did you want, Sharon? The alimony's not due till next month."

"I didn't call for money. I'm calling because of Paulie."

"Is he sick?"

"No ... yes, in the head a little, maybe. Phyllis had a cold last week, but she's better now."

"Yeah?" he breathed impatiently into her ear.

She'd be damned if she let his cud-chewing Irma get off that easily. And Barney, too, whose accidental spilling of seed eleven years ago had produced Paulie despite her pleading with him to put on a condom. Deciding against further stalling, Sharon let him have it all in one unedited rush. "Your son is on the verge of being turned out of the last day camp that would have him. And Rabbi Tayson doesn't want him back in school this fall, either."

"Why not?"

"He's a discipline problem, I don't know. I didn't talk to him, Pinnie did. Anyway, I'm going out there to see the rabbi about it tomorrow, do you think you can come?"

He made an indecipherable sound, and then seemed to disappear.

"Barney?" she thought she'd lost him for good then, their connection cut by the impatient Irma's hand. "Are you still there?"

"Yeah, I'm here." Barney muffled the receiver, permitting her to hear only the sound of murmuring. After a few seconds he got back on. "Listen, Sharon, I don't know why you bother me with these things. I have enough trouble keeping up with all the alimony you need. Where is it written that Paulie needs to go to a yeshiva? What do you want to do, turn him into a rabbi or something? You live in a good neighborhood. Let him go to public school like the rest of the kids."

Sharon was stunned. That little speech was the longest Barney had ever delivered in all the years she'd known him. She needed a minute in which to recover. "Is that how you feel about it?" she forced out, not sure whether she was about to laugh or scream.

"Yes, it is. Irma has two kids of her own, and I'll have to help out with them, too, come winter. And I'm no money machine. Besides, it's the slow season now anyway."

"Oh, yes, I remember." Though she tried hard to disguise her rage by tightening her quavering voice, she could not, so she took the next best way out: "Oh, my God! Soup's overflowing the pot! Sorry, Barney, gotta get off this very minute!" Hoping it would leave him at least partially deaf for life, she slammed the telephone receiver into its cradle.

It wasn't until the next morning as she was preparing to leave the house that, imagining Barney and his ruminant Irma interrupted while watching *The Price is Right*, Sharon saw the humor in that telephone call.

She was still three long city blocks away from the yeshiva and was already exhausted. Her feet were hurting. She wanted to sit down on one of the benches under the mealy canopy of trees lining Eastern Parkway and rehearse what she was going to say to Rabbi Tayson, but every bench she approached was torn to splinters. The neighborhood had fallen into such decay that very soon not even the Center's yeshiva could safely remain there. No doubt about it, this was no neighborhood for a yeshiva, or any kind of school, for that matter. Hence the urgency of Rabbi Joachim's fall fund-raising campaign. Should Leon Berkowitz, one of the Center's main wealthy donors, fulfill his promise to relocate the Center entirely to L.A., all their problems would be over. Poor Leon, lying with his bandaged knee up in the air at Lenox Hill Hospital.

Arriving at the yeshiva's front entrance, Sharon adjusted her headscarf and prepared her most convincing suppliant's smile for her talk with the formidable Rabbi Tayson. Just as she was about to take the first of the steps leading to the building, a huge brown dog rushed up ahead of her, barking furiously.

"Hush. Get out of here, you."

Leaping away at the sound of her voice, the dog gave her a mournful glance before loping down the steps into the street and disappearing around the corner.

If I believed, really believed in omens, she thought, what would I make of that one? As she stood there pondering the possibility that she only might have imagined the dog, she was interrupted by the deafening blast of a bell. Within seconds, boys of all shapes and sizes wearing identical white shirts, black pants, and black yarmulkes barreled past her in every direction. Desperately, she searched for Paulie but could not find him among them.

"Sorry missus," a little boy no older than five called back at her over his shoulder after stumbling over her shoe.

Sharon opened the front door and followed the boy into the building. In the hall, she passed three Ultra-Orthodox teenagers flaunting *tzizith* and long *payos*, who covered their eyes with their hands so as not to look her in the face. The little snot-noses!

She climbed the creaking wooden stairs to Rabbi Tayson's office fortifying herself with a list of complaints about the day camp: the hallways were dark and dangerous, there was dust everywhere, and the so-called playing field in the back was filled with dog poop and garbage. There were only four counselors out there managing a writhing mass of fifty boys. And they had been trained to discipline the younger, smaller ones by slapping them around, which, even for private religious schools, was against the law.

She reached the third floor. Walking past a storage room, she saw two bearded men in shirtsleeves stacking prayer books in neat little rows. One of the men let loose a ferocious sneeze that almost knocked her over. To her left there was a darkened classroom that smelled oddly of fresh tar. Down a long stretch of tiled corridor ending in a triptych of doors, Sharon found herself in front of Rabbi Tayson's glass-windowed office. It was there that her complaints about the yeshiva's dirty conditions failed her. Turning the knob with a trembling hand, she opened the door.

* * *

RABBI MORDECAI TAYSON HAD A REPUTATION for being a devious martinet who had come to the Kabbalah by default. Five years before being appointed principal of the Yeshiva Shimon Bar Yohai by Rabbi Joachim, he'd been headmaster—and the key figure in two scandals—at Derech Emet, a rather large and prosperous yeshiva in Borough Park. The first scandal had been minor, gaining no publicity beyond the parties involved. The second had been serious enough to make the newspapers and cost him his job. The trouble began when the school's accountant discovered that Rabbi Tayson had diverted funds designated for student scholarships to a down payment on a two-family house two doors away from the school, in which he'd hastily deposited his wife, four children, and in-laws. On being discovered, the rabbi immediately threw himself on the mercy of the school's board of trustees. A vote was held, the result ending in a tie. The Modern Orthodox members of the board wanted to give him another chance while the Ultra-Orthodox faction voted to fire him immediately. Their spokesman, Herbert Kravitz, the seventy-five-year-old owner of a chain of *glatt* Kosher barbecued-chicken stores, argued that the rabbi's admission of guilt was nothing but a ploy designed to keep his job *and* the house. Mr. Kravitz went on to warn that this would not be the end of what he called the rabbi's "machinations." Not one female member of the community was asked her opinion, but this did not stop the women from rallying in favor of Rabbi Tayson. Led by the Kosher butcher's wife—who was loath to lose a valued customer like the Rebbitzen Tayson—they pressured their husbands to give the rabbi another chance. As a compromise, the Ultra-Orthodox faction agreed to reinstate him on a trial basis. Except for an occasional complaint about his overuse of corporal punishment, the first year of the rabbi's probation passed in truce. Eventually, people lost interest in the affair. Several board members died, others left for retirement homes in and around Miami, and the angry Herbert Kravitz moved out of the neighborhood without telling anyone where he was going.

On resuming control of Yeshiva Derech Emet, Rabbi Tayson immediately set about implementing changes. One school committee after the next was proven to be an unnecessary expenditure of time and money. Jimmy, the porter of twenty-two years, was suddenly fired without severance pay. The entire English faculty was given notice and new teachers were hired to replace them. Parents were informed by letter that the Rebbitzen Tayson (who, it was later discovered, had never earned a teaching certificate) would be teaching three Hebrew history classes in the coming fall. A new dress code was announced: long sleeves, skirts, and headscarves were to be worn by all female teachers and visitors—Ultra-Orthodox or not. Yarmulkes were to be worn at all times by boys and men. Corporal punishment was to be administered at the discretion of each teacher, and Rabbi Tayson had the last word on all decisions relating to expulsion. The school sign was mysteriously repainted overnight; a brass weathercock was placed on the roof; and an intricately wrought matching brass door knocker (valued by a local hardware store owner to be worth seven-hundred dollars) was clamped to the massive front door—all of this without consultation from the school's Board of Trustees. Sunday classes were formed, and students—especially boys nearing the bar mitzvah age of thirteen—had to furnish parental notes in advance in order to be excused from Sabbath services. No English at all was to be spoken during the morning Hebrew session—not even at recess periods.

The community at large was too stunned to react. Except for one irate mother whose son had been suspended from school for refusing to stop speaking English, no one dared to confront Rabbi Tayson. But when the boy's mother actually found herself face to face with the rabbi, the poor woman was too intimidated to do anything but blubber into her handkerchief, "You're just a principal of education, not the boss over everything here." And her son was duly expelled.

Still, the rabbi was not without his critics.

"He's too Orthodox for my taste," the vice president of the ladies' auxiliary whispered in the ear of the treasurer at a luncheon to which Rabbi Tayson had appointed his wife keynote speaker.

"He's so religious he won't even look in a woman's face. Must be afraid we'll eat him up," clucked the treasurer.

"Probably didn't come to the luncheon for that reason."

"Sure."

"And she's a big snob, holds herself very high in her own opinion."

Then, in the breezy, leaf-dappled shade of a fall afternoon, the Tayson regime came to a sudden end. Once again, it was the women who, though not consulted, were responsible for re-ordering events— only this time they were arrayed against him en masse. It all started when a stiffly smiling ad hoc committee of three members of the ladies' auxiliary confronted him on the steps of the school. Elected by a majority vote of the membership, they were: a Modern Orthodox plastic manufacturer's wife (who, it was rumored, transgressed against the commandment to observe God's day of rest by watching television on Sabbath afternoons); the mother of the school valedictorian, whose brother, a graduate of *Derech Emet*, was studying for his doctorate in engineering at Bar Ilan University in Israel; and the auxiliary's outspoken vice president.

Confronted on the steps by the ladies' auxiliary representatives, Rabbi Tayson ended the recess period of four seventh-grade classes with one shrill blast of his whistle. The callousness of this dispatch convinced at least two of the ad hoc committee members that the rabbi was a tyrant who had, in the most sanctimonious of bloodless coups, taken complete power over the school for himself. (Their report to the ladies' auxiliary would later result in the addition of twenty-two women, increasing the ad hoc committee from three members to twenty-five.)

The vice president immediately came to the point. "You won't last two more weeks!" she said, looking directly into the rabbi's face.

Stunned by her disrespectful tone, Rabbi Tayson almost fell off the steps. Who was she, a woman, to be addressing him like this—and in public, no less? What insolence! Did she know she was talking to the man who had almost been appointed dean of the grand Theological Seminary of Baltimore? Never mind that the last-minute denial of his application had almost killed him. Never mind that his neck chafed daily at the collar of humiliation he was forced to wear as the lowly principal and self-titled headmaster of the Yeshiva Derech Emet of Borough Park.

Rabbi Tayson cleared his throat and prepared to respond; then, thinking the better of it, he turned his back on the vice president of the ladies' auxiliary and walked into the building. He was sure of one thing at least—the support of his handpicked teaching staff. Men like Otis, Abrahamson, and Knipfel *owed* it to him for taking them on without their teachers' licenses. They were an Ultra Orthodox crew, accustomed to taking orders; they would stick by him, he assured himself over and over again, turning his velvet yarmulke around on his head as he paced the seven feet of space between his enormous pine desk and the window overlooking the schoolyard.

Another week had hardly passed before two of Rabbi Tayson's most loyal secretaries gave notice. They were followed by a flock of teachers—both licensed and unlicensed. The ad hoc committee, now grown to forty, called for the rabbi's resignation in a two-hundred-and-fifty-dollar ad in the Brooklyn section of the *Jewish News*. Allowing him no quarter, the vice president lobbied in favor of his immediate expulsion. Several more temperate committee members recommended that the rabbi merely be docked at half pay and given time to find new employment.

On seeing the ad, the Rebbitzen Tayson fainted and was rushed to the hospital. She was released the next day with a diagnosis of severe stress and a prescription for Valium. The rabbi alternated between public fury and private bouts of weeping.

At a meeting called by the desperate Rabbi Tayson in his own living room, combining the all-female ad hoc committee and all-male board of trustees, two community elders got into a fist fight over a Talmudic ruling that was only vaguely related to the case and broke an expensive Israeli-crafted lamp. The rabbi pleaded for a second chance.

"Never! It's too late," screamed an otherwise docile pharmacist's wife, brandishing her fist.

The Rebbitzen Tayson broke down and was led sobbing from the room, and the meeting ended.

The Tayson children did not escape the fray either, and were mocked and tormented daily by their schoolmates. Discipline at Derech Emet was in a shambles.

At the end of its tether, the ad hoc committee agreed to seek the advice of the rabbinate at large. While the board of rabbis was in session, however, a group of militant parents, vowing to tear down the school brick by brick with their bare hands if Rabbi Tayson stayed on, pooled their funds, bought the storefront bingo parlor used weekly by the Derech Emet ladies' auxiliary, and promptly prohibited "all forms of gambling."

The factions grew louder and the rifts wider. Overnight, friends were estranged, in some cases, transformed into bitter enemies—even to the point of walking out on one another during the Sabbath service memorial prayers for the dead.

The petitioned Board of Rabbis—of which Rabbi Albert Joachim was then a member—decided on a compromise. Rabbi Tayson was to resume his duties as the school's principal until a new rabbi was found to replace him. During that time, he would cede all pedagogical decisions to the Board of Trustees. Proper channels were to be established for the school's building, financial, and hiring policies by an elected council of community leaders. A furor ensued the ruling. And more fist fights. Women were rumored to be spitting in each other's faces at the Kosher live chicken market. The whole Orthodox Borough Park community appeared to be running amok.

Impressed by the quiet strength he sensed in the man, Rabbi Tayson, without notifying anyone but his wife, privately sought Rabbi Joachim's counsel. It was during that meeting in Rabbi Joachim's cluttered office—before his practice of mystical Judaism became public—that the association between the two men was formed. In the case of Rabbi Tayson, it was less an association than it was an outpouring of gratitude and the pledge of a lifetime's devotion. To Rabbi Joachim, the enlistment of his first American disciple signaled the unofficial opening of a new era for the age-old wisdom of the Kabbalah.

On the advice of Rabbi Joachim (who in healing Rabbi Tayson's wounded ego had presented him with the opportunity to rule the Yeshiva Rav Shimon bar Yohai as he chose), the man who had come to be known as "the dictator of Borough Park," stepped down. The community was appeased, but only momentarily, for within a month of his departure, Rabbi Tayson was again at the center of controversy. This time, however, the charges could not be proven before a rabbinical court. It began with a series of morbid coincidences involving the rabbi's most vociferous opponents and did not end until every last one of his accusers had been afflicted. The vice president of the now defunct ladies' auxiliary set the spiral spinning when she lost her only son in a commuter train accident. The husband of the second-most prominent spokeswoman in the ad hoc committee lost his business and was forced to declare bankruptcy. The man next in line for Rabbi

Tayson's job developed cancer of the larynx, and so on, until even the minor characters in the drama had been stricken by misfortune. There were murmurings among the women about the "evil eye," and some even took to wearing red thread bracelets against its malefic influence. In their sermons, the neighborhood rabbis warned their congregations against indulging in forbidden superstitious practices, specifically admonishing the women for resorting to amulets. The gentler sages spoke of the Almighty's never-ending fund of compassion, while their fiery colleagues emphasized His judgment, but neither seemed to have any effect on their female congregants. Among the elderly women seated high up in the balcony rotundas of the synagogues or behind the screens separating them from the men, words like "plague" and "retribution" and even "witchcraft" were whispered. Many of the younger women, who in the past hadn't paid much attention to the services, began to engage in serious prayer for the first time.

Over an outdoor roast chicken picnic at Bear Mountain Park, the interim Board of Trustees, now composed entirely of members who'd had nothing to do with the Tayson affair, voted to put the Derech Emet yeshiva building up for sale, and to disband. As soon as the property was sold and transferred (to a young, innocent, red-cheeked Catholic priest, it turned out) and the building converted to a church--in fact, on the very day that a cross replaced Rabbi Tayson's weathercock on the roof--the neighborhood misfortunes ceased.

EIGHT

SHARON HAD LEARNED OF RABBI TAYSON'S unsavory past from Henry Novalis in hastily gathered bits and pieces. Rabbi Joachim had quickly put a stop to the gossip before she was able to get the whole story, but that hadn't prevented information from filtering through; the Rav Shimon Bar Yohai yeshiva was already rife with rumors about Rabbi Joachim's second-in-command when she'd enrolled Paulie. It was no secret that Rabbi Tayson's students didn't like him. Nor did his cold, disapproving manner endear him to the yeshiva staff. As far as she could tell, Rabbi Tayson had few followers outside of the small group of devotees who attended his Tuesday morning "Introduction to the Zohar" classes at the Center.

Still, Sharon did not want to think badly of Rabbi Tayson, or of anyone else connected with the Center—which Rabbi Joachim had described to her as the physical embodiment of the Kabbalistic Tree of Life, its descending branches representing levels of spiritual development. To reinforce his point, after expressing his disapproval of Henry Novalis and warning her to keep away from him, Rabbi

Joachim had her type up and post an announcement on the front-hall bulletin board stating that students of the Kabbalah were to refrain from gossip. Particularly in her role as his secretary, he warned, Sharon had to be careful to hold herself above the chatter circulating around the Center. After that, not even her strong desire to befriend one of her classmates, the curious, lantern-jawed Sylvia Hersh, had pressed Sharon into revealing information about Rabbi Tayson to anyone. She had to work especially hard to avoid the continuous questioning of Blossom Shatz—a notorious yenta and major competitor for Rabbi Joachim's attention—who, flaunting the Center's rules, polished her fingernails bright red, and then, in misappropriated acts of repentance, made a show of ladling out tiny portions of pilaf and string beans for herself on meatless weekend meditation retreats at the Leon Berkowitz estate in the Catskills. If there was one thing Sharon had learned from the Tayson affair, it was that gossip, like the evil eye, inevitably came back to harm its source.

Rabbi Joachim's Center for Mystical Judaism had opened a new world for her, and she did not have the right, she felt, to pick at its flaws like some other members did. Yet, she wasn't naïve enough to imagine that everything would be perfect once she'd joined. Institutions springing up around great religious leaders couldn't be expected to reach the spiritual level of their founders. She subscribed to her teacher's view of the Center as a series of descending and ascending branches of the cosmic Tree of Life, with Rabbi Joachim on the uppermost branch, and the other aspirants—including herself—located closer to the Earth in which it was rooted. With this image always in mind, she could forgive most of the petty transgression around her. Even the holier-than-thou smirk of Miss Axelrod, a children's book illustrator who had drawn a perfect replica of the stages of consciousness as described by Rabbi Joachim in a recent lecture, eliciting his initial, but short-lived rush of praise. Sharon had put the chart away in a file cabinet at the Rabbi's instructions.

"Not really very accurate, do you think?" he'd said, scrutinizing the illustration at arm's length and, as usual, not waiting for her to answer.

Rabbi Joachim's secretary could not allow herself to get sucked into the vortex of Center gossip, nor, in her hunger for friendship, could she allow the somber, lantern-jawed Mrs. Hersh to pump her for fiscal information or the voluptuous Blossom Shatz to sigh in her ear about "Albert's sex appeal." Though tempted at times to commiserate with these women, she remained aloof to their probing and innuendos, while at the same time, refusing to criticize them.

* * *

"Please sit down, Mrs. Berg." Greeting her from behind his desk, Rabbi Tayson addressed her formally as the mother of one of his yeshiva students rather than as Rabbi Joachim's secretary. "So sorry I don't have a more comfortable chair for you. We're in the middle of our summer inventory, as you can see," he pointed to a chair blocked by the disarray in her path: books piled high against an iron footlocker, prayer shawls, their tassels knotted beyond untying, a basketball, and an air pump.

Sharon sat down in the dusty high-backed chair he'd pointed out to her.

"Yes, I saw the men in the—"

"What do you intend to do with the boy in the light of my report," Rabbi Tayson interrupted before she could finish.

Battling a surge of nausea, Sharon struggled to maintain her composure. She'd never been good at showing respect for Rabbi Joachim's closest disciple, and his blunt assault caught her off guard. There was no getting around the arrogant picture he made sitting there in his funereal black suit and vest with that superior smile under his sly black mustache, his pudgy, soft hands forming a steeple against his ample belly. Avoiding the oily puddle of his glance and silently reiterating her pledge not to argue with him, she said naively, "What report?"

A long, dagger-like shaft of sunlight fell against Rabbi Tayson's left cheek. There was a slight flurry of movement on his side of the desk, a scraping of wheels, and an almost imperceptible shift in his position. Without getting up from his chair, he had turned to the window behind him and closed the blinds.

This is it, Sharon thought. Now he's got me dead to rights.

"Did you know, Mrs. Berg, that your son Paul is being evaluated by a child psychologist at my recommendation?"

She did not, but it was a rhetorical question, so she kept her peace and waited for Rabbi Tayson to continue.

"Did you know that Paul likes to duck his friends' heads in the toilet bowl of the boys' bathroom?" The rabbi tapped his fingers steeple against his vest.

So the interview was to take the form of her son's catalog of horrors. Sharon leaned her head thoughtfully to one side.

"Were you aware that he spits out the window at passersby during morning prayers? And that he has on numerous occasions left the schoolyard without permission in order to follow Catholic nuns down the street?"

Sharon was not aware that there were any other kinds of nuns in Brooklyn.

"As his mother," the rabbi continued, "I'm sure you'll be interested to know that he sometimes does not show up in school at all? And maybe you haven't heard yet that he was fresh to Rabbi Joachim during the bimonthly school inspection?"

"What did he say?" Sharon asked timidly.

"He said, 'I hate your guts,'" Rabbi Tayson said, leaving her open-mouthed. "Fortunately, Rabbi Joachim is a tolerant man, especially with children."

"Yes, extremely tolerant," Sharon murmured, looking down at a loose button on her dress. It was the sixth button down; she'd have to ask Pinnie to sew it back on for her, since she was planning to wear the dress to court on the nineteenth. She looked perky in that dress, it was shorter than most of her other clothes, a hand-me-down from Arleen. Junior would like it.

Seeing her drift off, Rabbi Tayson homed in for the kill. "Showing that kind of disrespect toward our founder is a very serious offense, wouldn't you agree, Mrs. Berg?"

Sharon watched the basketball roll and come to a stop at the tip of Rabbi Tayson's pointed black shoe. Or had she only imagined it?

"I'll have a talk with him."

"I already have."

"And?"

"The situation, I'm afraid, is very grave, very grave indeed." Unlike Rabbi Joachim, Rabbi Tayson did not roll his *r*s; they simply fell from his tongue like drops from a leaky faucet. "You are aware, of course, that it is only because of your unique position at the Center that I have gone to such lengths to keep Paul with us here. As it is"—the rabbi paused to touch his mustache—"at great cost to the yeshiva, in view of the waiver you are getting on his tuition, the virtually free summer day camp services—"

There was a knock at the door. "Hello, yes?" the rabbi called out.

The door opened and one of the bearded men Sharon had seen stacking books in the store room stuck his head in.

How convenient, Sharon thought. She didn't doubt for a minute that Rabbi Tayson had planned this interruption. She had only to look at the man awkwardly standing in the doorway to get the picture.

"Brendel, Fortzman, whatever your names are," the rabbi said to them, "come here, I want to talk to you for a minute." The group of bearded men entered. There was some deferential shuffling among them, with the tall sneezer stepping out in front of the short one.

"Rabbi?" asked the tall man.

"A lady is coming to see me this afternoon. One of you, make sure to knock on my door after fifteen minutes. I don't want her to over-stay her time and ruin my schedule. There's too much work to finish around here."

A grunt from the tall bearded one was followed by a chorus of "Okay, Rabbi." They paused, staring at Rabbi Tayson.

"Yes?"

"Rabbi, you told me to remind you," said the tall man.

"Thank you, Brendel, you can close the door now," Rabbi Tayson said, dismissing the bearded men from the doorway and loudly clapping an open desk drawer shut. Then leaning forward with an expression of feigned sympathy, he said, "I'm sure you understand my position. After all, Mrs. Berg, considering your own involvement with the Center—ahem, pardon me." The rabbi coughed a raspy little cough, covering his mouth with one hand and withdrawing it again, "I'm sure you comprehend the difficulties."

What was he up to? Where did he think he was taking her?

Thinking fast, Sharon pulled a handkerchief from her purse and dabbed at her eyes. "I fully understand your predicament, I really do. In fact, I only came here today to tell you—I came to tell you that I've thought it all out and I've decided that it would be better for everyone involved if I sent Paulie back to a public school in my neighborhood.

In fact, he's already been enrolled by his father," she lied, pretending to blow her nose.

"But what about his Hebrew education? Surely, you of all people would not want to leave him in the hands of—of *outsiders*, would you?" Rabbi Tayson rose up in his chair.

"If you mean *gentiles*, you needn't worry, Rabbi. It's a very Jewish neighborhood, the school is over eighty percent Jews," Sharon lied again, pulling numbers from the air. "It's one of those progressive schools, not more than ten children to a classroom," she added, knowing full well that at the Shimon bar Yohai Yeshiva for the children of mystical Jews, students were packed thirty-five to a room.

"Our master will be very disappointed in you," Rabbi Tayson parried quickly.

Sharon blushed. So he knew how she felt about Rabbi Joachim. The contemptuous smile on his face told her so.

"I don't want to inconvenience anyone with my personal problems," she said lamely. The conversation was getting dangerously out of hand. "Least of all, Rabbi Joachim." That, too, hadn't come out right; she was stumbling, falling fast.

"For *you*? Come now, I'm sure he'll be willing to make an exception. Hasn't he always, where you're concerned?" Rabbi Tayson cocked an eyebrow at her.

"What do you want me to do, then?"

"Five dollars a month," he shot at her crassly, looking at his watch.

She was wrong, the basketball hadn't move so much as an inch from the base of the footlocker. She'd only imagined it.

Rabbi Tayson riffled through the papers on his desk to let her know he was finished with her. "To defray the cost of the psychologist," he said without looking up.

"Three dollars," Sharon snapped back.

His neck reddening above his stiff white shirt collar, the rabbi said, "Very well, then, three dollars, if that's all you can afford at this time. We are well aware of your devotion to—to the Center, and we wouldn't want to be too harsh about the money. Nonetheless, the boy *is* a problem and needs special attention."

"I'll talk to him," Sharon said. She stood up and began to head for the door.

Rabbi Tayson likewise got up from his chair, walked around the desk and—as Rabbi Joachim never would—clasped her hand in his.

NINE

WITH PINNIE HOVERING OVER HER mopping up imaginary crumbs, Sharon sat at the kitchen table reading a book on Chinese medicinal plants.

"Well, what's it to be?" Pinnie had stopped pretending to clean the table and was standing in front of her with her hands on her ample hips.

"What are you talking about?"

"Paulie, that's what."

"He stays in," Sharon said, without looking up from her book.

"What did you do, twist Tayson's arm?" her mother laughed coarsely.

"Shush, I'm reading."

"All of a sudden I've got an intellectual for a daughter. If you're so smart, why aren't you rich?"

Seeing as her mother was in a good mood, Sharon thought it better not to tell her about the three-dollar-a-month tuition fee. In the dim hope that everything would work itself out on Rabbi Joachim's return, she dismissed the problem of getting the extra money from Barney. The most important thing was that her son would remain at day camp. Sharon's lingering anger over her conversation with Rabbi Tayson had caused her to reprimand Paulie more harshly than she'd intended, and he'd responded tearfully, "Barney doesn't care about us anymore, and Grandma Pinnie likes Phyllis better than me. I wish you were home more often, Mama, you're the only one around here who cares about me."

Guiltily acknowledging her son's wise assessment of her motherly shortcomings, she'd kissed him on the ear and recklessly increased his allowance by a dollar. Though bribery had never been her preferred way of dealing with Paulie. Nor was substituting junk food and toys for love. In fact, Sharon had always loved her son more *because* he was difficult, not in spite of it. And because he reminded her of her tempestuous father, who'd referred to himself as an "unfinished symphony" lacking the patience to finish what he started—not even managing to stay alive long enough to guide her away from the perilous, crooked paths of love. She and Barney had already been sleeping in separate beds by the time Paulie turned five. A late attempt at reconciliation had resulted in Phyllis being born. But by then it was clear that no amount of patching would fix the tear in the marriage, and Paulie had borne the brunt of it. Sharon tried her best but had failed utterly at shielding him, and later Phyllis, from the anger and resentment she harbored for Barney. By withdrawing and leaving their mothering to Pinnie, she'd unintentionally leveraged her rage on her children instead. Now she feared it was too late to undo the damage.

Later that afternoon, while Pinnie played cards with a neighbor, she took her book on Chinese herbs out to the porch where she could read while snatching glances at Phyllis asleep in her stroller. At four o'clock, after Pinnie had returned from her card game, Sharon went to the Center to check for telephone messages and found only two—both from telemarketers. With Rabbi Joachim gone, all the life seemed to have been drained from the office. Except for a heavier layer of dust, nothing had changed. The bathroom window sash was still stuck, and the same green rim of grime still circled the drain in the sink. Even a plastic spoon under a pile of sooty receipts remained where it had been carelessly stashed and forgotten three weeks before. Saddened by the emptiness of the place, Sharon quickly pocketed the mail and went home to give herself a permanent. When that didn't improve her mood, she impulsively bought a black and brown spotted Basset Hound puppy she'd seen pining in the window of a Coney Island Avenue pet shop—only to return it two hours later. Too much time on her hands was making her reckless. Unable to stand being alone any longer, she called her sister and suggested they go to a movie. Arleen said she was busy but invited Sharon out on a double date the next night. Arleen's boyfriend Les would bring along his friend Dave for Sharon. She reluctantly agreed to meet them on the southwest corner of St. Mark's Place and Second Avenue.

* * *

EMERGING FROM THE SUBWAY UNPREPARED for the sultry squalor of the East Village on a summer night, Sharon held her breath as she hurried past a barefoot derelict lying facedown on the sidewalk. At the Cooper Square traffic island, a group of teenaged panhandlers pleaded with her for change. When she waved them away, a beautiful porcelain-skinned blond girl told her to go fuck herself. A policeman sitting on a horse nearby heard her and laughed, then turned his horse in the opposite direction and trotted off, leaving an enormous pile of turds behind him. Never mind, Sharon thought, unlike the derelict or the teenaged panhandlers, you at least have Pinnie, an apartment in a house on a tree-lined street, children who are still too young to panhandle, and thanks to Rabbi Joachim, a spiritual life. Then, as if her master were mocking her for her smugness, a hollow-eyed girl who could have been Paulie's age accosted her.

"Please, miss, I haven't eaten for three days, please, miss, please."

Dropping a dollar bill into the girl's outstretched hand, Sharon hurried on, breaking into a run past a leather shop and a food stand where a withered slice of pizza rotated on a tray under a red bulb.

Arleen, who had promised to wear a skirt, was dressed in blue denim overalls and a white t-shirt, which meant that in her high-heeled shoes and tailored blue linen suit, Sharon was overdressed. Never mind. She'd barely been introduced to Dave and was already sorry she'd come. When she'd asked him his last name, he'd laughed in her face and refused to tell her.

"Are you wanted by the police?" Sharon asked sarcastically.

Dave laughed again. "Not that I know of, but you gotta be careful. Never tell your full name to anyone on the street."

Dave's furtive eyes matched his paranoia. His other notable characteristics were a shiny pink bald dome that was not unlike Barney's except for some long, scraggly side hairs that he had gathered into a ponytail and tied with a leather thong, stale cigarette breath, and tobacco-stained fingers.

Arleen, whose tastes had never included men in suits, had surprised Sharon by hooking up with Les, a portrait painter by choice and textile designer by necessity, who, despite the heat, was wearing a corduroy suit. Arleen had always thrived on contradictions.

The four of them were standing on the corner deciding where to go when a a woman leading a Great Dane on a short leash stormed out of the candy store behind them.

"Honky, honky dirt!" she hissed. "Overcharging me 'cause I'm black, that's what!" Then, stopping in her tracks only a hair's breadth from Les, she screamed, "What you lookin' at, white man? You got somethin' to say to me, you say it, hear!"

"I wasn't looking at you," Les was foolish enough to yell back at her.

A small knot of onlookers gathered around them. The dog's mouth hung open, disclosing a long pink tongue lathered with drool. Excited at the prospect of seeing the beast unleashed and Les mauled, three skateboarders began goading the woman on. At that moment a quartet of policemen emerged from a patrol car parked across the street.

"Move along, move along, nothing here for you to see. Let's go!" Brandishing nightsticks, they dispersed the crowd and spoiled the show.

Sharon was instantly reminded of Officer Pols—and then, of Junior Cantana.

"How about a Chinese movie?" Dave asked as they headed downtown. "I hear they're full of gorgeous naked Oriental chicks and cool samurai violence."

"Samurai are Japanese," said Arleen.

"I'll see anything," said Les, wedging himself between the two women.

"How about you, Sharon?"

"Huh?" Dave's question had caught her in the middle of remembering Junior Cantana at Coney Island karate-kicking Jorge Diaz into the sand.

"Do you want to see a Chinese movie?" Arleen asked pettishly.

"Anything you decide is fine with me."

"Don't be so wishy-washy, Sharon. Do you or don't you want to see a Chinese movie?"

"Sibling rivalry already, and the evening's only just begun," Les chuckled.

"Oh, never mind," Arleen said, waving her hand in disgust. "You won't get a straight answer out of her anyway. You never do." She pulled Les ahead, leaving Sharon and Dave to fend for themselves.

When they couldn't find four seats together in the crowded Chinatown movie theater, Dave volunteered to take the last two empty ones in the front row. Furious at him for not consulting her, Sharon pulled away and scrunched into the farthest corner of her seat with her head tilted upward, pretending to be absorbed in the swordplay on the screen. Feeling another migraine coming on, she'd lowered her head and was just starting to nod off when she felt Dave's fingers digging into her thigh. Sitting this close to him and breathing the same stale air had been bad enough, more than Arleen had the right to ask of her. "All in the spirit of good sportsmanship," a phrase Arleen had thrown at her as kids, playing to Sharon's childhood terror of "not being fair" to her younger sister. But this went beyond fairness. The first man's hands on her body after Barney not to be those of Rabbi Joachim—it was too much to bear. But no, she was wrong; Dave wasn't the first—only three days ago Rabbi Tayson had given her a clammy handshake.

"Please stop," she whispered, pushing Dave's hand off her thigh.

"Loosen up, girl."

"No."

Dave hardened his grip. "Come on, Sharon don't give me that virgin crap. Arleen told me you were divorced. You know what it's all about, baby."

Sharon looked around to see if the man sitting next to her had heard them. But he was slumped against the back of his seat, asleep with his mouth open.

"Please, I mean it," she said urgently, again trying to loosen Dave's grip. He was digging his fingers deeper into the flesh of her thigh, hurting her. (In a parallel drama on the screen the movie's heroine, a frail Chinese princess, was being assaulted by a loathsome, beetle-browed villain.)

"No, you don't understand me," Sharon whispered loudly.

Dave angrily got up from his seat and headed for the lobby.

Sharon was on the verge of leaving when he returned with two jumbo bags of popcorn and handed her one.

"Peace offering," he mumbled, seating himself stiffly at a distance from her.

Sitting there quietly eating her popcorn, Sharon mused on her inability to walk away from men who treated her badly.

The movie ordeal finally came to an end, and Arleen, Dave, and Les stood in front of the theater debating where to eat. Sharon stood apart from them watching a Chinese couple with a sleeping baby in a pouch slung over the man's chest share a bar of sesame candy.

Arleen broke away from Les and Dave to inform her that they'd decided to pick up some Chinese take-out and eat at Dave's place.

"I can't go; I have to be in court tomorrow," Sharon shot back quickly.

Arleen gave her a sour look.

"Told you she was a narc," cried Les, laughter turning his eyes to slits.

"Court?" Arleen snapped. "You never told me anything about having to go to court. What about that job you're married to? Does that maniac boss of yours even give you time off for court?"

"Jury duty, I have to," Sharon stammered, now desperate to get away.

"Jury duty? You mean to tell me that people still go? Tell 'em you're a housewife, and they'll excuse you. I know everything there is to know about jury duty. I was even on a jury once myself—saved a spade's ass," Dave chortled, taking her arm.

Eyeing the creepy late-night hordes and beer-sloshing men sprawled on the surrounding tenement stoops in their tank tops, Sharon relented.

The men led the way, each of them carrying a plastic bag stuffed with Chinese take-out containers. As they walked along Avenue A, Sharon noticed that a group of firefighters had just finished hosing down an abandoned car that had been set ablaze.

"Here we are," Dave called out, oblivious to the smoky aftermath of the fire. "Home at last." Unlocking the bolted door of what looked to Sharon like an abandoned factory, he led them into the dimly-lit front hall and up three flights of stairs to his apartment—a cavernous warehouse with floor-to-ceiling plywood shelves crammed to bursting with old LPs, books, magazines, cardboard boxes, tools, and every imaginable synthetic and natural material for drawing, sawing, sculpting, hammering, and building. Enormous worktables were strewn with half-finished projects made of balsa wood; geometric paper models were propped up to catch the light cast by bulbs painted blue and orange and red. Dave flipped a switch and activated three chartreuse and indigo light-boxes he'd fashioned from discarded or stolen X-ray screens; a shimmering frenzy of strobe lights; sewing machine parts; electro-cardiograms featuring blood-red heart failures in a grotesque variety of zigzag patterns; a cacophony of rotary telephones set to ringing at intervals.

Les threw himself down on a ticked mattress pressed against a wall. "This is great, man, really cool," he said, clicking his tongue against his teeth.

At Dave's invitation, Arleen flipped a switch and, to her delight, set off another miniature light show.

Sharon sat down stiffly on the edge of an empty juice crate facing the mattress.

"Anyone want beer or wine with dinner?" In his own domain, Dave had lost his cynical demeanor and grown affable, gathering his guests around the mattress, doling out the food and drinks, making sure not to let Sharon's container of vegetable lo mein get mixed up with the shrimp and pork dishes after she'd timidly informed him she was Kosher.

"Can you turn some of those lights off?"

"What's wrong, do my light shows make you nervous?"

"No, but, but," Sharon had no intention of telling Dave that blinking lights gave her migraines. Spotting a record album lying open on the floor, she chose to divert him instead. "I haven't seen an LP in ages and you have such a great vintage album collection; I thought it might be nice to listen to one of your records."

"Did you set up the stereo system yourself?" Arleen had switched off the light show and was now surveying the speakers hung in every corner of the room.

Dave picked up the record album Sharon had pointed to and placed it on the stereo player.

They scare me—all three of them, Sharon thought. Even my sister.

"I'm technologically oriented, as you can see," Dave grinned.

"Man, that's an understatement!"

"How much wattage does this take?"

"About a hundred and fifty volts."

"No kidding?"

"Looks like a dump from the outside, but it's Oz in here."

"Have you exhibited any of your work?"

"I didn't see any light boxes nearly as good as yours at the Electronic Age Show."

They babbled on, leaving Sharon to hum along in her increasingly woozy head to the LP's synthesizer version of Bach's Brandenburg concertos. Her second glass of wine was starting to give her a buzz, and Dave's toys reminded her of the circus, Sunday afternoons at Radio City, and all the other good times she'd had with her father. She got up and wove her way toward a door marked W.C.

Hunched high above the toilet seat, she peed, flushed, and washed her hands. Lingering so as to avoid unnecessary contact with the trio beyond the W.C. door, she studied the strips of photographic negatives Dave had hung from clips lined up along the naked shower curtain bar. Then she spent five minutes staring at her face in the toothpaste-stained mirror over the sink, recalling the Sunday her father had tipped a chubby museum matron with wrinkled elbows to take her to the ladies' room to pee. The matron had lifted Sharon to the sink so she could wash her hands. "What a lovely little girl, and such good manners, too. You ought to be very proud of her," the woman had crooned to Sharon's father upon returning his daughter to him.

"I *am*," Daddy had brushed aside his cowlick and taken Sharon's small, sweaty hand in his. "I'm *very* proud of her."

When Sharon emerged from the toilet she found Arleen and Les entwined on the mattress, watching three TV sets simultaneously. On a twelve-inch black-and-white Sony, the Braves were playing the Red Sox; a twenty-seven-inch Panasonic was showing John Wayne in *The Quiet Man*; and a reconstituted Phillips portable was presenting a rerun of *The Ed Sullivan Show*, which had gone off the air the year before. The volume on all three TV sets had been turned down, and a hot guitar was providing background music.

"Django Reinhardt?" Les called out, disentangling himself from Arleen and sprawling out on the mattress. He laid his head in Arleen's lap.

Dave stood off to one side rolling a joint in American flag-patterned cigarette paper. "Right you are, my man! And for that, you get a reward." He licked and pasted the paper seam and handed the joint to Les.

"I get clairvoyant when I smoke pot," Arleen said.

"This is where I get off," Sharon made her way to the table near the front door where she'd left her purse and scarf. No one seemed to have heard her. But that didn't surprise her; she'd been talking to herself all evening.

"It's hot as hell in here, can't you either turn on a fan or open a window?" Arleen asked before taking a drag on the joint Les had passed on to her.

"Never, my dear lady," Dave answered. "Never een zees illegal pad do we open zee windows, for zey are nailed shut, *mon cherie*. But wait!" Now playing the scrappy French magician, he slithered over to a window covered by a pair of black-painted Venetian blinds, and, pulling them open, revealed an air conditioner.

"Voila! Built in by yours truly, and hooked up like all these private, unbilled telephones here, to the Con Edison electric company free of charge," he boasted, turning on the air conditioner full blast.

"Wheee! That's what I call conning the cons!" Arleen giggled. Now fully stoned, and a little drunk from the wine, her face had puffed up under her Granny glasses and her straight Dutch-boy hair had gone limp.

"Sure you won't have one for the road, Sharon?" Dave was leering at her.

"I said no, thanks."

"Leave her be, my sister-the-goody-two-shoes. Always the goody-two-shoes."

"I told you it's those quiet ones you gotta watch out for," Les said, lifting his head from Arleen's lap and switching TV channels. "They're the ones that always turn out to be the narcs."

"I'll just leave this with you if should have any use for it in the future," Dave dropped a joint into Sharon's bag on his way to the stereo.

Here she was, talking about going to court and she might get busted herself, creating a scandal for the Center, destroying any chance for—

"*Fool,*" she suddenly heard Rabbi Joachim chiding her, "*I'm barely gone a week and you let yourself be taken over by the Other Side. What good has all my teaching done for you?*"

Dave placed a new record on the turntable. "Guess this one!" he called to Les.

"This is terrific shit," Arleen said. She yawned and removed her glasses, exposing a bright pink scar under her left eye.

Suddenly transfixed by the memory of how Arleen had gotten that scar, Sharon stood in the middle of the room, tying and untying her scarf.

"*You did that to her,*" Rabbi Joachim scolded her. "*Remember how you fought, tossing chairs at each other—at Passover, no less—with Pinnie pleading with you to stop; your grandmother cowering near the cupboard.*"

Of course I remember, Sharon thought. How could I forget smashing both fists into my sister's eyes, throwing her to the floor, pinning her down with my knee to make her stop taunting me.

"Swear you'll shut up and I'll stop. Swear!" she had screamed at Arleen.

"Sharon's got a boyfriend, his name is Jake. Sharon pulls his pants down to kiss him on the snake! Ha! Ha! Ha! Ha! Ow! Ouch, stop it!"

Arleen wouldn't leave off taunting me, Sharon remembered, not even with the cut opening under her eye, the blood gushing.

"You stop it!"

But Arleen wouldn't stop. She laughed all the way to the hospital and continued taunting me through the four painful stitches they gave her. I was the one crying hysterically throughout my sister's ordeal. I was the one who had to be sedated.

"Going home so soon?" Arleen called out in her old taunting voice.

"Hey, don't waste that!" Les sprang forward to retrieve the flag-wrapped joint that had fallen from Sharon's open purse as she pulled the strap over her shoulder.

"This is boring—boring and childish," Sharon heard herself say. The wine buzz was almost gone.

"If you don't like it, you can fuck off, bitch," Dave pushed her roughly toward the door.

Sharon turned to Arleen for a sign of sisterly protection, and got none—which, in light of her own past transgressions, she realized, was exactly what she deserved. Arleen was curled up like a cat on the mattress, smoking her joint with one hand and stroking Les's hair with the other.

"What are you waiting for?" Two hard fists nudged Sharon between the shoulders. "Beat it!" Dave opened the door and, pushing her out into the hall, slammed it shut behind her.

Feeling her way downstairs through the darkness, Sharon stumbled out of the building and fled westward, toward the lights, through the wild, siren-blasted streets, running, until, waving her hands around like a mad woman, she stopped a cab that had just turned the corner and nearly run her down. She didn't know if she had enough money to get her all the way to Brooklyn. But she didn't care. She had to get home to Pinnie and the children, where she belonged.

TEN

EXCEPT FOR A MAUVE-SKINNED MAN in a peaked cap and a woman in sneakers wearing heavy black lisle stockings, a dirndl skirt, and peasant blouse, her Medusa hair festooned with ribbons, Room 104B seemed to be filled with the same people Sharon had seen the first time she'd come to court. Only today they appeared to be less criminal than demented. As she took her seat beside a worried looking Officer Pols, even the avuncular judge, in his black robes, looked sinister. No sign of Junior Cantana.

Sharon had barely sat down when she was called up to the bench and informed by the clerk that Jorge Diaz, once again, had not turned up to face trial. Momentarily disoriented, she wondered whether she hadn't invented the whole purse-snatching story, conjured up Junior Cantana in her despair over Rabbi Joachim's desertion. Why else would she have come here?

"It's because you're attracted to the goy, that's why you keep coming back," Rabbi Joachim leered at her from the bench.

"And why isn't the defendant present?" the judge asked angrily after ordering Sharon back to her seat.

A young moon-faced lawyer wearing thick glasses jumped to his feet. "Your honor—"

"Yes?" the judge toyed with his gavel as if threatening to clobber the lawyer with it.

"Mr. Diaz refuses to cooperate with his court-appointed attorneys. He won't speak to anyone but his mother and keeps demanding new lawyers."

"Have you tried getting him a lawyer who speaks Spanish?"

There was a brief rustling in the aisle as Junior Cantana took his seat next to Sharon. "Sorry I'm late. I borrowed a car and couldn't find a parking space," he leaned over and whispered in her ear.

The judge tapped his gavel.

"Silence! Silence in the courtroom, please," ordered the security guard from his post near the window.

"Will counsel kindly inform Mr. Diaz that he has the right to a fair trial with any attorney he chooses, but that this is not an end-of-the-season-sale," said the judge, hunching his shoulders and revealing his fleshy pink neck. "Have Diaz in this room on Friday at ten, counselor," he roared, "or you'll hear from me! Case postponed."

Junior Cantana smiled at her, provoking an unaccountable twinge of pleasure. Officer Pols, she noticed, was sitting in the row in front of her, muttering. No, she hadn't made them up. They were real. They were here.

When, in his weary voice, Officer Pols asked if Sharon would come back to court on the following Friday, she agreed immediately. Nice couple, he thought as he climbed into the seat of his patrol car next to his bull-necked partner of four years. She's a little taller than he is, and probably has a couple of years on him, but they're a nice couple anyway.

"Onward, Charlie," he said.

"Problems, eh?" Charlie was looking out the window at a well-endowed legal secretary in a peppermint-striped, backless halter-top and was sweating profusely despite the air conditioning.

"Nah. Everything's okay." Officer Pols removed his hat and sighed. At least that nice couple will have a chance to get to know each other better after this—they're decent people, he thought. Then placing his hat over his eyes, he leaned back and drowsed as Charlie wove the patrol car slowly through the narrow streets of Little Italy.

* * *

FOR THE SECOND TIME IN TWO WEEKS, Sharon found herself standing next to Junior Cantana on the courthouse steps. Crime, it seemed, had become their only legitimate excuse for coming together. But she was not really surprised, for, like her fraught relationship with Rabbi Joachim, this one, too, was tipped with a dollop of cosmic irony: the man was younger, shorter, and not Jewish. Shrugging her negative thoughts aside, she walked with Junior toward his borrowed car, a shiny new cream-colored Volkswagen Beetle with a ticket fluttering softly against the windshield in the fetid breeze of a passing bus. The meter had expired, its red tongue sticking up at them spitefully. Of course, Sharon thought, how could it be otherwise?

"I'm sorry, it's probably my fault," she said. "I'm like that cartoon character, Joe Bitzflick, do you know him?"

"Yeah, he's the little guy with the perpetual cloud over his head. But the ticket isn't your fault; it's mine. I didn't put enough money in the meter."

"No, no, it's me. I'm a jinx, if there ever was one. Better get rid of me now, unless you like courting disaster."

"How can you be so sure it isn't me who's the jinx, and that you're not the one who's courting disaster?" Junior asked archly.

Sharon wished she could just shut up. Why was she turning a simple traffic ticket into a cosmic disaster? Why wasn't she like one of those women who'd see the whole thing as an adventure and joke about it? Or laugh and punch him on the arm? Suddenly afraid she might do just that, she sprang away from him.

Junior didn't seem to have noticed. "Can you beat that?" He pulled the ticket from the windshield. "It's seventy-five dollars!"

"Don't pay it. You have a Pennsylvania license plate. You're from out of state," she said, hurrying after him as he jogged back to the courthouse.

The judge had just declared a recess and was heading down the narrow staircase leading from the bench to his chambers when Junior intercepted him.

Sharon stood to one side watching dust motes tumble through a ray of sunlight over their heads.

"Just give it here," the judge said in a loud voice, taking the ticket out of Junior's hands and tearing it in half before disappearing into his chambers.

"What was that all about?" she asked as they left the courtroom, this time letting Junior take her arm as he led her through the crowd in the corridor and out of the building.

"All he needed to hear was that I'm a wounded vet," he said, giving her a wry smile.

* * *

EXCEPT FOR A LONE POLICEMAN drinking coffee, Hardy's Luncheonette was empty. A woman in a wraparound apron with

SUPERB printed on the front had replaced the droopy-eyed counterman and was spooning rice pudding into single portions from a large glass bowl. Looking up and seeing Sharon and Junior enter, she directed them to a booth and asked them for their order. The waitress was nowhere to be seen.

"Two coffees, please," Junior called across the table to the woman behind the counter. Then, turning to Sharon, asked, "Do you really want me to go through the whole boring story?"

"Yes, everything."

"But why?"

"Because I like stories, any kind. Even boring ones."

"Well, thanks a lot for not mincing words."

"And tell the truth," she added eagerly.

"What makes you think I wouldn't?"

"Just checking...go on."

The counterwoman brought their coffee.

Junior took a sip. "Okay, I come from Norristown, Pennsylvania, from a family of working people. My father was a firefighter, but they retired him in 1970, and now he tends bar on the West side of town. Dad's happy there. The job gives him a chance to hang out with his cronies. My mom worked all her life as a cleaning lady at the local high school. She used to bring stuff home all the time—scraps of geometry paper, the unused halves of notebooks and colored pencils that the kids left behind in their lockers at the end of the term. That's how I started to draw—copying Mickey Mouse from comic books, stuff like that.

"Once, my mother brought home a pair of sneakers for Dom, my older brother, but he said he didn't want to wear any secondhand sneakers, so she gave them to me. I've never been too proud to accept seconds. The sneakers were too big, but I saved them till I grew into them and wore them to Scout meetings. My father was Scout Master then, and president of the local American Legion post. I think he still is. He fought in Korea. He and I used to go out on hikes in the Poconos, did all the typical father-son things—roasted potatoes on a stick over a fire—and fought like a pair of wild dogs. We had different opinions about everything, especially politics. Dad came to this country from Naples as a kid with nothing but the clothes on his back. He's so grateful for what America gave him that you can't criticize anything about this country without getting an earful. He thought I was too radical, so he made me enroll in ROTC my first semester in Community College. My mother was totally apolitical. She had only one dream in her life for me—that I become a priest.

"We had a dog, a big black mongrel called O'Dad because Dom would always say, 'Oh, Dad!' when my father told him it was his turn to mow the lawn on a Saturday morning. O'Dad's still around, he's nearly blind now, with one game leg. Dom was like my dad, a real gung-ho guy. He joined the Marines as soon as he got out of high school. Went off and got himself killed in Vietnam.

"I did all the typical things Italian kids do in Norristown—played football and busted windows for a lark. One boy—his name was Carlo, too, but he shortened it to Carl—carried around a pair of brass knuckles and had an uncle in the Mafia. He'd cruise the black neighborhoods in his father's Buick looking for fights, but nobody ever obliged him. Having no one to fight with, Carl got so bored that he killed himself with an overdose of heroin. The Norristown paper didn't talk about it much, but there were plenty of white guys shooting up in those high school bathrooms my mother was cleaning. The idea that someone my age could really die shook me up, especially after going to the wake and seeing Carl lying in his coffin, dead, with his hair parted on the wrong side. I hadn't actually seen Dom get killed, so it didn't hit me so physically at first. Then, after getting the whole story from a Marine who came to the house with my brother's dog tags wrapped in an American flag, I got this picture in my head of Dom crawling through the jungle, lost, wounded, looking for help. Nights I'd wake up screaming because I had this recurring dream that he was buried in a swamp, but still alive, and I was on the verge of pulling him out. Then he'd get sucked under and disappear. Mom would come running into my room to calm me down. She'd talk about how I wasn't going to be like my brother, how I'd bring peace and joy to people as a priest—not death and destruction. I really think she was a pacifist without knowing it. Anyway, she lit a lot of candles to the Virgin for me and saved up for my college tuition by working extra hours as a babysitter for the G.E. physicists living in the townhouse developments around the industrial park.

"Mom is what you would call 'big-boned.' She let her hair go gray naturally, never dyed it, never changed her hairstyle; she still wears it in a braid, folded up on top of her head. Hard work keeps her alive. She's never been happy with my father. He treats her badly when he's drinking too much beer, and when he's sober he doesn't talk to her at all. She was pregnant with Dom when they were married. You'd think being a cleaning lady she'd have no energy left when she got home, but she always kept our house neat, everything always in its place. Mom wore her white uniform around the house because she was always on the verge of going out to work somewhere. She'd stick this funny blue velvet ribbon in her hair, and when you asked her why she wore white sweat socks over her nylon stockings, she'd say it was to protect her shins when she scrubbed floors. No mops for her, she wasn't satisfied unless she got down there on her knees and polished them by hand.

"On Sunday, off would come the uniform and on the print dress and purple lipstick, the straw bonnet with the cherries, or the blue felt hat with the feather on the side. After church, Mom and her sister

Katie would meet with their Italian-American clubwomen at Arby's on Route 202 for a pot roast lunch. One of them was an astrologer who joined them every other Sunday and told their fortunes. My mother stopped going when Dom died. Losing him was awful for her, and then having me come back wounded must have pushed her over the edge. She's let the house go to pieces; there's paint peeling off the ceiling, wet laundry hanging from the backs of chairs in my father's room—they don't sleep together anymore—and the kitchen is filled with empty cereal boxes, pie tins, three-day-old bread from the local thrift bakery. Mom's become a pack rat and refuses to throw anything away. She says that if *her* mother could see the condition of our house, she'd be rolling over in her grave. But she doesn't seem to be able to do anything about it. It's as if she's given up—on everything. I tried talking her into seeing a therapist, but she wouldn't even listen to me, just turned her head away and changed the subject. My aunts have given up on her too. Nobody talks about Mom's depression anymore when the family gets together at my uncle's pizza-joint in Bridgeport—that's the town right before Norristown.

"As for me, I ran wild after Dom died. When I graduated from high school I went to work in a nearby carpet mill because I was convinced I needed the money to buy a car. Don't ask me where I was planning to go, I had no idea. All I knew was that I wanted a car, even if it meant only looking at it in the driveway or hosing it down on a Saturday. As soon as Mom found out I was working in the mill she came right down there and yanked me out by the collar of my shirt. I was almost glad she did. The nap from the carpets would get into your throat and stick there like a package of dried breadcrumbs with the cellophane still on them, and you were always wheezing and blowing your nose. Many of the people who'd worked there for years developed T.B. or lung cancer later on.

"If I couldn't have a car, I decided that I had to have *something*, so I went out and got myself tattooed on the leg. I wanted it on my arm, but I got the tattoo on my leg so my parents wouldn't see it. Dad probably wouldn't have cared but Mom would have gone nuts. Imagine, a priest with a tattoo! I couldn't think of anything in particular I wanted, so I chose the picture of the first billboard I passed, and that was an ad for a summer theater version of Tennessee Williams's *The Rose Tattoo*. The coincidence impressed me, I guess, and here I am with a rose tattoo on my leg."

Bending over, Junior lifted the left leg of his pants and showed it to her. Oddly, rather than being disgusted, Sharon was fascinated.

"Were you sorry you did it?"

"Not at all, I even thought about becoming a tattoo artist myself. But my mother acted even faster on that idea than on getting me out of the carpet mill. I'd been taking courses at Norristown Community College after graduating from high school, and since my grades were good, my counselor advised me to apply to college after my first year there. I'd made a half-hearted application to Villanova and forgotten about it. But one day I came home and found that I'd been accepted. You can imagine how Mom reacted, and before I knew it, I was a theology major heading straight for the priesthood. At Villanova I developed a passion for drawing and—unfortunately for my mother—a huge distaste for religion. Art and theology never mixed for me; they still don't. I took honors in every studio class, even pulled an A minus in sculpture, gobbled up a thousand years of art history—and flunked all my other courses. They put me on probation, gave me aptitude tests, the works. For one semester the school even paid for me to see a shrink twice a week. He was a nice old Viennese guy, a Freudian type in a vest with a watch chain—just like the shrinks in the movies. On his report to the probation committee he advised against the priesthood for me and recommended I switch my major from theology to art. He was a good man, Dr. Berkan. Too bad he died of a heart attack right in the middle of the faculty dining room one afternoon—over an untouched cup of tomato soup and a cracker.

"On the doc's recommendation, the committee let me stay on through my sophomore year. I worked like a fiend, trying to prove myself. I became art editor of the school newspaper, but they dumped everything else in my lap as well—writing, drawing, printing, you name it. Not that I complained, mind you. It was a terrific opportunity for me, a real proving ground. I started a cartoon strip of my own for the sports page, made up a character called Harvey the Hoop, and was soon satirizing the bigwigs on campus in the guise of a basketball net. From there I moved on to politics, scouring the papers, reading every political cartoon I could get my hands on. I'd found what it was I wanted to do with my life, and nothing was going to stop me. I had my mind set on it. Until then it had all been a blur. Then, wouldn't you know it; I was thrown out of school once and for all. They simply couldn't keep me on with my failing grades, they said, because I was taking the place of a more deserving student who would pass all his courses, and not just the ones he liked.

"For a few months after that I just bummed around. The mill had closed and work in the area was scarce. Even the physicists at G.E. were being laid off. My mother was crushed by my failure and wouldn't even talk to me. My father, who couldn't care less, sat around reading the American Legion News, with one hand always firmly wrapped around a beer bottle. Every so often he'd look up and curse out the 'pinko priests' at Villanova as a kind of cold comfort to her, then he'd look at me and say something like, 'Why don't you join the army and become a real man for once in your life?'

"'Sure, a dead man, like his brother,' my mother would answer for me. But by then, even she didn't seem to care what I did with my life.

"I spun pizza dough in the window of my uncle's place in Bridgeport until the smell of tomato paste and basil drove me back into the streets. At night, with O'Dad snoring on the studio couch next to me, I'd sit in my room drawing cartoons. Within four months I'd covered enough paper with political satire to fill a portfolio for the F.B.I. My father would have been the first person to report me, I'm sure, if he ever saw what I was drawing in secret. During the day I'd study karate, flirt with the waitresses at the Route 202 Diner, or just sit in the public library reading art books. When Mom stopped supporting me, I enlisted in the Marines. That was before the Tet Offensive, and I wasn't even thinking about being sent to war.

"At Fort Pendleton, where I did my basic training, I became a medic. That's a story in itself, but I'll save it for some other time. From there it was only a hop, skip, and a jump from California to Da Nang, to getting a sniper's bullet in the stomach while evacuating three wounded soldiers, to being shipped straight to Walter Reed and becoming a recovering war hero. Once I was on my feet, they sent me home to Norristown—the last place, I would have chosen myself. One advantage, though, is that my parents don't bother me anymore. The other good thing about all this is that I get my honorable discharge in October, with the Pentagon paying for twenty-two months' worth of missed art lessons.

"From there, I'm on my own. I'll probably take a job on a paper somewhere in Podunk, live in a barn, and draw anti-war cartoons to my heart's content. Eighteen months in Vietnam has given me more than enough raw, firsthand material to start with," Junior signaled the woman behind the counter for more coffee. The policeman had gone, leaving them with the luncheonette entirely to themselves.

"There it is in a nutshell." Junior spooned sugar into his coffee then handed Sharon the shaker. "What about you?"

"You didn't tell me how old you are," Sharon said.

"Guess."

"I'm not good at guessing people's ages."

"I'm twenty-eight," he said quickly.

"I thought you were still in your twenties. Would you like to see a movie?"

"Where did that come from?"

"It just came up out of nowhere, I guess."

"Sure, but not before you tell me *your* story. I'm not letting you off so easily now that I've bared my soul."

"Tit for tat," Sharon laughed, and quickly turned red at having used the word 'tit.' "Okay," she added, hoping he hadn't picked up on her embarrassment, "I'll tell you my life story after the movies."

"It's a deal."

"Let's go."

"Remember, though, it's your turn after the movies."

"I promise."

"Good, let me pay for the coffee first. Hey, do you even know what you want to see?"

"No, but I have two free passes to any Fox theater in Brooklyn."

"Well, then, who cares what's playing."

Sharon put on her sweater.

"Won't you be too warm in that?"

"No, I get cold in air-conditioned theaters. They always turn it up too high."

"I'll keep you warm," Junior said.

Pretending not to hear him, Sharon stifled a smile.

They left the luncheonette and were walking toward the car when she touched him on the shoulder and blurted out, "I'm desperately unhappy," the words pouring out of her mouth before she could stop herself.

"Is it your family?" Junior put his arm around her and caressed her cheek with the tips of his fingers.

Mortified by her outburst, Sharon shook her head. "Let's not talk about it now, she murmured. "Later, you can come home with me after the movie."

"Sure."

"Do you have to bring the car back?"

"Not until tomorrow. It belongs to my friend's wife, she's a nurse."

"Are you having an affair with her?"

"Of course not! Really, Sharon, you say some weird things."

"That's only one of the things Barney hated about me."

"Barney?"

"My ex-husband. He's marrying someone named Irma this winter. She's a gum snapper. I just thought you might like to meet my mother and kids, but you don't have to come home with me if you don't want to."

What *dybbuk* had taken possession of her and was driving her to talk to him like this?

Junior pulled her closer. "Don't worry, Sharon. I'm great with mothers and kids."

ELEVEN

PINNIE WORRIED ABOUT WHAT SHE CALLED "the weirdness" her daughters had inherited from their father. Sharon had been twelve and Arleen ten when he died, too young to do anything but glorify him—especially his favorite, Sharon, the one he proudly called "my first-born" and whose head he'd fill with crazy stories before disappearing for days on end. She'd never really gotten over the shock of his permanent absence. Unlike Arleen, who'd raged and screamed when George died, Sharon had numbly retreated into silence.

George Kellner—aspiring writer and failed husband—may he rest in peace. Pinnie had married him after only two months of dating—if sitting in a rowboat on Central Park Lake listening to George lecture her on everything from Aristotle to Zen could be called "dating." Occasionally she'd put in a word or two, but mostly she listened. She'd fallen in love with him almost as much for his formidable intelligence as for his looks, his smooth-skinned oval face and burning black eyes. In contrast to her own placid, easy-going sensuality, George was nervous and driven, consumed by goals and aspirations that were never to be fulfilled. He'd charmed her by reading his scribbled journal notes to her at the oddest times, compelling her to stop what she was doing and listen to the jumble of philosophy, economics, doggerel, and plots for detective novels he intended to turn into films. George's imaginative and wide-ranging interests continued to stoke her desire for him even as their marriage faltered. Pinnie accepted the paradox presented by her husband, even after she'd confronted him and he'd admitted to his affair with a Venezuelan dyer in the shoe factory on Greene Street where he worked as a foreman.

It was on a cold winter evening during one of his extended absences from home—when she presumed he was with his lover—that George either jumped or fell to his death on the tracks at the Greene Street station of the Lexington Avenue subway. As soon as she got the news, Pinnie decided to tell her daughters that their father had died of a heart attack. Why further complicate an already complicated situation?

As for herself, she had no desire to marry again, one husband like George was enough. Besides, widowhood afforded her a newfound independence that, except for the cash-strapped state in which George had left her, she rather enjoyed. She could now polish her nails silver (which he'd hated), slip into one of the full, open-collared rayon dresses he'd called "cheap looking," eat a whole box of almond-nut-honey chocolates if she wanted to, and spend her afternoons playing canasta with her neighbors. George had tried to expand her mind with books and classical music, and Pinnie had resented him for it. She'd had no idea how much she'd resented George's efforts to educate her until the tragedy on the Lexington Avenue subway put an end to them. It was like having an iron bar removed from her chest. The only thing she'd been afraid of was that his Venezuelan mistress might turn up at the funeral, but to her relief, the woman stayed away. In the weeks following George's death there'd been a few times Pinnie thought of telling her rival off to her face, but by spring the impulse had passed and she became her old, cheerful, easy-going self again.

Pinnie was sure that her younger daughter, Arleen, was, like herself, a survivor who would make her way. But Sharon seemed headed for an especially hard ride. Like her father, she wanted too much out of life. Living with George had taught Pinnie that such desires were doomed and that the disappointment they carried with them could be fatal. She also knew that despite her own motherly efforts to soften the blow, Sharon would have to confront her disappointment alone—hopefully, not in the way her father had. In the midst of bathing and diapering Phyllis, or mixing milkshakes in the blender for Paulie, Pinnie grieved for her afflicted daughters. Maybe it was her fault for trying too hard to protect them. Maybe she'd done the wrong thing by lying to her daughters about George's death, or by keeping his affair with his Venezuelan mistress a secret—even now that they were grown women with a right to know the truth about their father. But Pinnie had missed her chance. Arleen was hardly on speaking terms with her these days, and Sharon was far too fragile.

Pinnie had once hoped that husky, round-shouldered Barney Berg might inject some normalcy into Sharon's life. True, she'd had her misgivings about his being fifteen years older, yet, knowing that Sharon was one of those girls who needed a father substitute for a husband, she'd kept her misgivings to herself. But the promised salvation in Barney's adoring glances had turned out to be illusory. There were the fights to put up with, the frantic calls interrupting Pinnie's canasta games, when, ashamed that her friends might overhear Sharon's screams, she'd turned from them and whispered into the telephone, "I'll be there. Just give me twenty minutes."

"Another emergency?" Yetta Solow had pressed her thumbs to her sagging cheeks, barely suppressing the glee in her voice.

"No, just one of the usual minor catastrophes—one of the kids fell off a chair and they need me to watch the other one while they drive to the hospital," Pinnie said, overcoming the urge to slap her ill-wishing neighbor in the face.

"Ah, they never stop needing their mamas, not even when they become mamas themselves," said the good-natured Flo Kaplan tipping back in her chair and popping a caramel in her mouth. "God bless them. Here, I'll play out your hand, Pinnie. I've got nothing in mine anyway."

The "emergencies" were inevitably followed by Sharon's futile attempts to explain why Paulie was wandering around the house barefoot, entangled in pajama bottoms that had fallen to his knees. Sharon had never learned to sew, and her kids' perpetually buttonless and zipperless condition were a testament to her marital disarray. The first time she'd been called to intervene, Pinnie had hurried up the stairs with her heart thumping, prepared for a replay of her own brawls with George. But here the roles were reversed: it wasn't Barney screaming and throwing furniture around, it was Sharon. Barney was sitting in a daze in front of the television set. When Sharon divorced him, Pinnie proclaimed her public approval. These days, alone, in private, she cried with her face in her hands at the thought of her vulnerable daughter's headlong flight into "Mystical Judaism." At Sharon's request, Pinnie had moved in with her and assumed care of the children—knowing even as she did so that she was positioning herself to buffer the heartbreak awaiting her daughter at Rabbi Joachim's hands—and that her efforts would come to nothing. Restrained by the glow in Sharon's eyes as she enthusiastically described her work at the Center for Mystical Judaism, Pinnie didn't have the heart to warn her of the crushing rejection that lay ahead. Instead, as she had in the rowboat with George, Pinnie sat quietly listening. Then one day she exploded. Her fierce mother's instinct wouldn't allow her to do otherwise. It was past midnight and she was heating Phyllis's milk at the stove when Sharon came into the house and walked past the kitchen without greeting her.

"So, now you're too high and mighty to even bother saying hello to your mother!" Pinnie yelled after her.

"Leave me alone, Ma, can't you see I'm exhausted."

"Sure you're exhausted. That fraud rabbi of yours has got himself a first-class pigeon."

"Don't go there, Pinnie, I'm warning you." Sharon had come back and was now standing in the kitchen doorway, shaking her finger at her.

"Don't you tell me where to go or not to go; I'm your mother! And I see what's happening. I see you throwing yourself away on that phony-as-a-two-dollar-bill crackpot rabbi of yours! Working like a horse for a pittance, spending money you don't have on seventy-five-dollar initiation fees and non-accredited yeshiva tuition. You're making yourself sick over a man who's just using you, can't you see!" Pinnie cried.

Sharon paused for a moment, the blood draining from her face as she fought to control her temper. In ominously quiet tones, she said, "The milk is boiling over. You'd better turn off the gas." As soon as she'd spoken, she left the doorway and went straight to her room.

Pinnie's hands were shaking as she turned off the gas and removed the pan of milk from the stove. She'd waited too long to warn her daughter of Rabbi Joachim's power to destroy her. She should have said something after his one and only visit, to "Kosher" the house, but she'd been too afraid of provoking a fight.

The children had been sent to Flo Kaplan's so as not to disturb the Koshering ritual, and there'd been just the three of them: Sharon,

Pinnie, and the rabbi—tall, lumpish, goateed, with a wrinkled brow, wearing a black hat that he never removed. Once he'd finished touring the house mumbling incantations and scalding the dishes and pots and pans in the kitchen, he'd stood in the middle of the living room scanning the furniture and the worn Moroccan carpet, frowning at the plastic forsythia in the cracked peanut butter jar on the coffee table. Pinnie was certain that the whole Koshering ritual was nothing but an excuse for the rabbi to assess Sharon's family finances and that his real purpose for coming had been to nose out a potential donor. She'd had enough experience with his kind from way back, in her mother's time: big-bellied, black-bearded rabbis smelling of musk and schnapps, selling holy trinkets at the door; vending prayers for the dead, obscurely creeping up on you in cemeteries from behind a loved-one's headstone with their dog-eared prayer books open to the mourner's page, their rancid breath on your face as they read the Kaddish "for a small fee, Missus, whatever you can give." Recently, from Yetta Solow, an ardent Israel supporter who traveled there twice a year, Pinnie had heard that the same bearded men in the black hats were selling prayers in Hebrew to American Jewish pilgrims at the Wailing Wall in Jerusalem, shamelessly begging for money even there, on holy soil.

But after spending an hour in Rabbi Joachim's company, Pinnie had changed her mind. Sharon's Kabbalah master wasn't at all like the black-bearded desperadoes who preyed on old women. In fact, he was like no other rabbi she'd seen before. A charlatan, yes, but no beggar. Crazy, yes, but like a fox. Instead of asking Pinnie for money before leaving, he'd offered a waiver on Paulie's tuition and hung expensive silver made-in-Israel *mezuzahs* in every doorway without asking for as much as a dime. From the way Sharon had looked at the rabbi as he tapped the mezuzahs into the lintels, mumbling in Hebrew with his eyes half-closed, Pinnie could see that her daughter was already too far-gone to be rescued. She was therefore totally unprepared when Sharon appeared in the front porch doorway under Rabbi Joachim's bulging silver mezuzah with a handsome young man who, introducing himself as "Junior Cantana," warmly shook her hand. Pinnie was so shocked by the uncanny likeness between her late husband George and the young man standing alongside her daughter that she couldn't open her mouth to speak, and Sharon had to invite him in.

Pointing a trembling finger at the brown wing chair (in her opinion, the best piece of furniture in the living room), Pinnie at last found her voice. "Sit down, I'll get you some cold apple juice. It's organic, just what you young people like, the best kind." She hurried toward the kitchen. "They advertise it on the radio every morning."

Junior settled into the chair and looked around. He was smiling at Sharon, making her want to run over and kiss him on the mouth again, as she had when they were sitting in the movie theater, holding hands in the dark. Not a good idea with Pinnie poised to come back from the kitchen any minute—but she'd really enjoyed that kiss. It had been good for her ego, if nothing else. Instead, she turned on the radio, stopping at a music station playing an Edith Piaf song in French. She cast Junior a suggestive smile. Pinnie was calling her from the kitchen in a suspiciously casual tone. There were bound to be the usual mutterings at the sink, to be followed by her mother's crudely spat out disapproval. Too bad, Pinnie, it's just too damned bad, Sharon thought, planning her attack as she backed out of the living room and headed for the kitchen. If only she weren't always forgetting to install a dimmer switch, she could have lowered the room lights. What was wrong with her? Had she gotten drunk on one kiss? Or was it because she was so eager to spite Rabbi Joachim for leaving her?

"Shit," Sharon's heel got caught in a loose flap of linoleum at the threshold and she nearly fell face-forward into the kitchen.

"Junior ... Cantana? What kind of name is that for a Jewish boy?" Pinnie asked, loudly slamming the refrigerator door so as not to be heard in the living room.

Reminded of Mrs. Wolstein by her mother's commanding tone, and then of Rabbi Joachim winging his way over the ocean through the clouds to bed his wife, Sharon said aggressively, "He's not Jewish, Ma, he's Italian, Catholic."

"Italian?" Pinnie repeated warily.

"Yeah."

Pinnie replaced the sweating bottle of apple juice in the refrigerator. Standing in one tiny square on the linoleum floor, with the deft and easy movements of her fading breed, she set three full glasses of juice on a tray without spilling so much as a drop, pressed three paper napkins into service, and arranged a platter of *Oreos* to serve alongside them.

"There!" she dusted her hands free of imaginary crumbs against the sides of her dress. "Just like you to catch me in my housedress and torn slippers. So how come you didn't call?"

"First of all, you don't have to stay up and wait for me. I'm not fifteen, and it's not my first date."

"I'm not prying, if that's what you think. I would have prepared something more substantial to eat if I knew you were coming, that's all. So stop devouring me with your eyes."

"Cookies and juice'll be fine," Sharon picked up the tray and walked out of the kitchen. When she was halfway into the foyer, she heard Pinnie whisper behind her, "He's younger than you."

"Yes, he is," Sharon resumed her suggestive smile without turning around to face her mother. "So what?"

"Nothing ... sew buttons," Pinnie joked lamely.

Junior was no longer seated when mother and daughter entered the living room. Standing with his back to them, he was selecting books from the shelves. He was even shorter than Sharon thought, but at that moment he looked like a giant, his head almost touching the ceiling. "Mother says the children are sleeping. You'll have to visit with them some other time."

"Gladly," Junior said, nodding self-consciously in Pinnie's direction. "It'll give me a good excuse for visiting here again." Embarrassed at having invited himself, he quickly turned his attention back to the bookcase. "Interesting set of books you've got here. Like *The Mystic Way*." He opened one of Rabbi Joachim's precious volumes and glanced at the Center's purple stamped address on the inside cover.

"What is this soldier, this Catholic from Pennsylvania, doing here in your living room handling my books, sacred works I've entrusted exclusively to your care!" the astral voice of Rabbi Joachim bellowed at her from behind the bookcase. *"Remember, Sharon, these are dangerous volumes containing secret symbols of the Jews, never, never to be profaned by the hands of nonbelievers!"*

Here, right this minute, before her eyes, a gentile intruder she herself had brought into her home was flipping through the precious pages of the Kabbalah. What had she done? Sharon dropped the tray roughly on the coffee table, spilling juice on the paper napkins and wetting the cookies. "But those books aren't mine," she cried desperately. "They belong to my boss!"

"Are you aware of the holiness therein? Make him put them down! Quickly!" No longer just a voice coming from behind the bookcase, the fully embodied astral Rabbi Joachim was now standing in front of it, his eyes boring into her.

"Those books have a lot of complicated symbols, things like that," Sharon explained to Junior. "They wouldn't interest you. My boss is a...a religious scholar doing research on—gosh, here I've spilled...give me...let me put the book back. You really wouldn't be interested at all."

Sharon flung herself at Junior, trying to replace the book and shove the glass of juice under his nose at the same time.

Ah, now what? Pinnie thought. Aloud, she said, "Well, folks, I'll be leaving you. I'm pooped and the kids will have me up by six-thirty, so..."

"Oh, don't go," Junior coaxed.

"Good night, Pinnie. Sleep well." Sharon waved for her mother to leave, but Pinnie wouldn't budge.

Mercifully, Rabbi Joachim had vanished.

"I can't stay very long anyway, I have to get my friend's car back," Junior said. He stood awkwardly in the middle of the room, waiting to be asked to stay a while longer.

Sharon rubbed the blister that had formed on her left ring finger, a white band circling where she'd worn her wedding ring. Now that the book incident had torn away what Rabbi Joachim called "the veil of illusion," she was disgusted with herself. The blister on her finger opened and began oozing lymph. It had started with a paper cut she'd gotten in the office on the day before Rabbi Joachim's trip to Israel. Seeing her wince as her finger began to bleed, he hadn't so much as offered her a Band-Aid. "A paper cut hurts most," was all he'd said, absent-mindedly looking past her.

Junior was shaking hands with Pinnie. Why hadn't her mother gone to bed yet? Why was she still standing there in her hideous carpet slippers playing chaperone? Why, after all these years, was she still meddling? Sharon fixed on the plastic-covered sofa as an emblem of all she hated about the house. Not a spot of dirt had rubbed off on it, not a dent, no dark, worn grooves where a man might have sat. She and Barney had lugged it home themselves.

"Too cheap to hire a mover!" she'd screamed, panting as she'd helped him heave the sofa up the porch stairs. "Too cheap, you're just too cheap for words!"

Barney had insisted on buying the sofa at an auction for twenty-five dollars.

"I wouldn't take that thing if they *gave* it away," Sharon heard a gray-haired man with a pipe sticking out of his jacket pocket say to his wife on the bench behind them.

Every piece of furniture in the living room had its own shabby history. Now Junior Cantana was standing in the middle of it, becoming part of that history, his feet planted on the spotted square of Moroccan carpet, his eyes moving from the La-Z-y Boy to the ancient oak coffee table, to the window seat that doubled as a radiator cover to the burlap curtains Pinnie had sewn herself and hung on thick brass rings—standing on a chair without any help from Sharon. The room smelled of mothballs and kids' vomit, and the plastic sofa covers had squeaked obscenely when Junior plopped down where Rabbi Joachim had refused to sit.

"Good night, all. Nice to meet you," Pinnie finally waddled off.

"I'd really better get going," Junior said.

Startled out of her reverie by his voice, Sharon gave Junior her hand. It was like loving him, bringing him home like this. Not that she really understood anything about love. Lust, maybe—yes, what she was mistaking for love was really lust. The radio's musical broadcast was interrupted by a perfume commercial followed by a station break, and a gong—in that order.

"I have a birthday coming in two weeks," she said, letting him pull her closer. "I'll be thirty-five." Someone else seemed to be speaking thickly from behind her face, using her voice. The announcement hung in the air between them as they stood facing each other in her tacky living room surrounded by reminders of her failed marriage and Rabbi Joachim's invisible presence.

"Sshh, a girl's not supposed to tell her age." Junior took her hand and pressed it gently. "Will you come and spend the weekend with me?" he murmured. "There's an inn...and farms...a picnic...my friends..." Sharon heard him say through the barrier in her ears caused by her pounding heart.

Lust, she thought. This is what I'm feeling now with him, not love. It's Rabbi Joachim I love. This is pure lust.

"Yes, I'll come," she promised.

Junior kissed her eyelids. The warmth of his breath, the scent of trees in the rain—Sharon let them enfold her then pushed him away. "Stop, no more now," she said hoarsely.

I'm afraid of what I want, she thought. Now he'll go home. Next weekend we'll be together. After that, Rabbi Joachim comes back and it'll all be over.

"We can leave right after court. I'll borrow the Volkswagen again. You'll meet them, my friends." Junior tapped her on the nose. "The woman you thought I was having an affair with. My friend's wife— you'll like her. We'll go on a picnic. Do you like horses? Do you ride?" Junior was breathless, too, stammering, fumbling in his efforts to convince her to take part in this thing that was enveloping them both so quickly.

Sharon felt his erection as he pressed her close to him. Again she pushed him away. This time, Junior let her push him out onto the porch. Watching as he walked down the cement path leading away from the house, she saw a thick-furred black tomcat stalking into the night behind him.

TWELVE

SHARON WAS SITTING IN THE FARTHEST CORNER behind the upper railing enclosing the Grand Army Plaza Library Rare Book Room trying not to feel guilty about her betrayal in accepting Junior's invitation to spend the weekend with him. She was using Rabbi Joachim's special scholar's pass, hastily scribbling notes on a long yellow legal pad from a pharmacopoeia of herbs that would ostensibly cure all but her own discontent. Despite the air-conditioning, it was so wickedly hot that the librarian had gotten up from her desk to switch on a standing fan in the opposite corner of the room. The fan blew the onion-smelling air around, flipping the pages of Sharon's yellow pad back and forth until she placed a book on top to hold them down. Two men in open-necked polo shirts who looked like plainclothes detectives were conferring near the dust-covered microfilm machine that no one had used all morning. Fearing that the plainclothesmen might take it into their heads to use the microfilm machine, the annoyed librarian, after returning to her desk and throwing a pink sweater over her shoulders against the draft from the fan, now sat frowning at them.

Sharon was the first person in the sparsely occupied room to notice an old man shuffle in, groping with palsied hands at nothing in particular as he threaded his way toward the open bookshelves like a beached turtle. Putting down her pen, clicking it shut, and pressing the soles of her shoes against the bar of the table in front of her, she settled back in her chair to watch the trembling old man. Taking down a book and opening it to what appeared to be dead center, he would mumble a few lines to himself, then, apparently dissatisfied, would shake his head, put the book back on the shelf, and start the procedure all over again. Having spent a good part of her life in libraries, Sharon was hardly moved by the old man's eccentric behavior. She'd seen much worse. It was only because she was tired of writing that she kept watching him. That was how she came to be the first person in the library to see the old man go white from the cross-hatched baby hairs on his head to the turkey skin at the opening of his shirt collar as he let the fifth book drop and slumped to the floor. Instinctively, Sharon rushed to the stricken man's side.

The old man was deathly pale but, thank god, he could still talk to her. His false teeth were clattering around in his mouth like a pair of castanets. *Take his teeth out!* Sharon vaguely recalled the words of a distant lifeguard at a hotel in the Catskill Mountains...a lake...her honeymoon. There, parodying the seriousness of her present situation, surrounded by flagstone and shrubbery and oiled brown bodies, one of the hotel guests, a laughing man with a hairy chest, had simulated a heart attack for a lifeguard's quickie course in First Aid. That distant summer afternoon, along with a host of other strange, unrelated images, tumbled through Sharon's mind as she bent over to help the old man. It was as if an invisible hand were flipping through a dusty family album she hadn't bothered to look at in years. *Most important is that you act quickly.* Sharon reached past the old man's parched lips and removed his bridge. At least he won't choke, was her final thought before calling out for help. Despite his weakness, the old man's clammy fingers were wrapped around her wrist so tightly that her skin was turning blue. He wore many rings, and the backs of his hands were covered in liver spots.

Fortunately, as it turned out, the two men in polo shirts were not plainclothes detectives but off-duty hospital aides. Spotting the old man on the floor and Sharon kneeling at his side, they hurried over to help. One of them told the librarian in the pink sweater to call for an ambulance while the other removed the victim's jacket and rolled it into a pillow, which he placed under his head. Searching for a medical bracelet, and finding none, he asked the old man if he was diabetic. The old man gathered enough strength to whisper back that he wasn't, adding that he'd smoked for too many years to give it up now, and that the doctor had been watching the old ticker recently.

"Did you take out his bridge?" the first hospital aide asked Sharon.

"Yes."

"Good. Now go and get some cold water and some paper towels; he's sweating." The more assertive of the two men had a blond buzz cut. His nose was thin and beaked, the skin on it nearly transparent.

Returning with the roll of paper towels and cup of ice water the librarian had handed her, Sharon noted that the old man had perked up and got some of the color back into his face. It was as if the mere presence of the beak-nosed hospital aide, his barking orders at everyone and expecting to be obeyed, had somehow convinced the old man to remain conscious. Everyone else in the room seemed equally impressed. Neither Sharon nor the snippy librarian had questioned his orders; even his colleague had submitted to the beak-nosed man's commands. Remarkably, only three minutes ago, they'd all been strangers, no contact between the librarian and the casual, nondescript men in the polo shirts, the old man on the floor, and Sharon. Now, guided by the beak-nosed hospital aide, they were a team intimately linked in a drama of life and death.

Dipping a wad of paper towel into the water, Sharon knelt beside the old man and sponged his veined forehead with it. Her hands and feet, her entire body, seemed to be moving of their own accord—infused by a strength she'd never known before. So this was what Rabbi Joachim meant by "spiritual power": Kneeling here on the floor next to a fusty old man among thousands of rare books, squeezing drops of ice water from her improvised poultice to his foam-flecked lips. Reaching for the roll and tearing off several more sheets, she wrapped the old man's false teeth in a dry paper towel.

"Ah...ah...that's good," he murmured brokenly, the corners of his mouth flecked with foam. Then pulling her down, he whispered into her ear, "I—I think I'm going to be sick."

Bringing the old man into a seated position, she pointed to the wastebasket alongside the librarian's desk; immediately, the meeker of the two aides got up and fetched it. Clearly displeased by the thought of the old man vomiting into her wastebasket, the librarian sprang into action. "Look here," she began waspishly, "just a minute—"

The beak-nosed hospital aide had only to look up to stop her in mid-sentence.

"I—I feel better," the old man said, leaning back. "It's passed. I feel better this way, lying down, I think."

"Guess you ought to think about quitting smoking Pop," the beak-nosed hospital aide said jokingly. "I stopped—took me, let's see... Harry?" He looked at his colleague and wrinkled his forehead. "How long is it now since I stopped smoking?"

Catching on to the game, Harry said, "Gosh, Phil, maybe three years. Yeah, I'd say three years."

Phil looked at Sharon and said, "How's about some more sponging for our friend Pop here, eh, Miss?"

By now the old man's color had returned to the point where his face no longer resembled a paraffin mask. The two men kept bantering and Sharon continued sponging the old man's forehead until the ambulance arrived. Tearfully thanking them for their help, he made the sign of the cross as he was lifted onto a gurney and rolled out of the library into the street.

Phil got up patting his pants pockets to make sure that nothing had fallen out of them, causing a crumpled package of *Camels* to fly out and land in the wastebasket. Harry bent over to pick up the cigarettes and the two hospital aides smiled at each other sheepishly.

"Ya gotta tell 'em *something* to keep their minds off it, right?" Phil said.

"Does the old guy have a chance, do you think?" Sharon heard Harry ask as the two men brushed past her without saying goodbye.

"Who knows? You never can tell with them tickers," said Phil without a trace of feeling, "especially at his age."

* * *

BACK IN HER CHAIR, Sharon tried reading her notes but could not concentrate because the incident with the old man had brought back memories of her honeymoon: the lake, the slick young bodies, Barney's yellow-checkered bathing trunks, the disappointment of their sweaty first night of lovemaking, but mostly the dreadful story of that afternoon kept pressing in on her. Too vivid as it was now, rendering her scrawls illegible, the story demanded—like a suitcase standing unopened in a hallway too long after the end of a trip—to be opened, and its contents properly stored away.

Sharon closed her notepad and slipped her pen into the pharmacopoeia between two glossy color sketches of St. John's Wort to keep her place. All right, she told herself, you can think about it if you want to—but only for five minutes. It was a "waking dream" exercise Rabbi Joachim had given her, designed to purge the mind of obstructive memories.

The Evergreen Lodge. I'm on my honeymoon, making my way to the lake to meet my new husband Barney. I walk through the red plush and cherry wood bad taste of the lodge's lobby and out the curtained French doors past the reception desk and the black studio piano that no one plays, narrowly avoiding the disheveled old man with the yellow walrus mustache, whom I like to think of as British. As I push the door open, the curtain flutters in the sunlight. I hurry down the fir-lined path and hear the screams of honeymoon wives being plunged in chicken-fights from the shoulders of their new husbands into the cold water of the lake. When I reach the lake, the first thing I see is the white wooden dock bobbing up and down in the black water on its orange oil drum anchors.

"Eeek! Barracuda!" a man shouts in a falsetto.

"Shut up, dope," a woman screams.

An oversized pink beach ball hits the water with a thunk. The lifeguard blows his whistle. I squat down and scan the water for Barney, my new husband, a sparse-haired ad salesman from the seventeenth-floor offices of the Belvedere Mill Corporation. Squatting on my haunches like this, I can stay put for hours, which never ceases to amaze Barney, who says he can't even bend over and touch his toes, his knees are so stiff. Barney is fifteen years older than me, but he is a strong swimmer, whereas I can only negotiate the water with a reluctant sidestroke.

On a rise above the cropped grass shoreline where the flagstone begins, serious sun-worshippers oil and grill their bodies on long, white chaise lounges, and cabana boys in red-white-and-blue boaters hustle for tips.

Mitzi Dorman, a blond interior decorator wearing an oversized pink straw coolie hat tied under her chin with a red sash, says, "Imagine using railroad ties for a sundeck. Wonder who thought that one up? What a savings..." Mitzi is talking to her bridge partner, a very fat woman in a muumuu. Mitzi is divorced, a stalker of other women's husbands. She drinks frozen daiquiris and uses the word "nifty" a lot. Her silver mandarin fingernails flash like mercury in the sun as she picks up and puts down cards, reminding me of Pinnie. On a nearby chaise lounge, with her rump up, sprawls Betty-with-no-last-name. Like the elderly "British" gentleman and Mitzi Dorman, Betty, too, is unattached, but Betty isn't looking for company. She arrived at dusk three days ago during a furious ping-pong match on the front lawn with only one suitcase and a pile of Vogues *under her arm. From her first day out, Betty has spoken to no one. She lies sunning her magnificent body, which she enhances by changing bikinis mornings and afternoons and by turning browner every day.*

The lifeguard blows his whistle again. He's a Princeton student, wearing an orange baseball cap with a miniature orange tiger embroidered on the brim. In the evenings, having changed into a blue blazer, white slacks, and sky-blue polo shirt, he dances with the unattached women at the lodge. Everyone but the lifeguard gets slightly tipsy before nine, when the comedian comes onto the dance floor and tells forty-five minutes' worth of dirty jokes through a hand-held microphone.

The lifeguard picks up his bullhorn and announces that a special guest, an intern from the local hospital, will give a lesson in first aid. I see Barney getting out of the water and wave to him. He is talking to Ed Mendelsohn, a spindly-legged insurance salesman. Greeted by a chorus of mock groans, the lifeguard shoos everyone out of the water. Betty-with-no-last-name never so much as moves a muscle. The intern, who wears his hair long and is dressed in hospital blues, winks at the lifeguard and tells everyone to form a circle. Still talking, Barney and Ed Mendelsohn join the circle. The intern asks for a volunteer who will simulate a heart attack, and a hairy-chested honeymooner in a Speedo steps to the center of the circle and lies flat on his back on the ground. His wife, a pony-tailed blond, immediately gets into the spirit of the demonstration by crying for help.

I feel the saliva welling up in my mouth. Barney is motioning for me to come over. His athletic supporter is sticking out of one leg of his yellow-checkered bathing suit. The intern says, "Seriously, though, Mrs.—"

"Robbins," says the 'victim's' wife.

"Right. Okay, then, Mrs. Robbins, what would you do first if you found your husband like this?"

"Take out his false teeth!" a man yells from the second row of the circle.

"Scream bloody murder, that's what I'd do," says Mrs. Robbins, making the crowd laugh. A few of the men appear to be on the verge of leaving.

"When you gotta go, you gotta go. That's my philosophy," says a man wearing blue espadrilles and smoking a cigar.

"Who started this, anyway?" a middle-aged self-described engineer on his second marriage asks irritably. His wife, a schoolteacher twenty years his junior, is pouting.

Under the intern's direction, the lifeguard gets down on his knees and presses the heels of his hands into the victim's hairy chest.

"Hey, boy," comes the muffled complaint. "Go easy there, will you? I'm not made of rubber."

A few people snigger, others cough self-consciously. The lifeguard demonstrates three different methods for applying artificial respiration. The intern says, "Mouth-to-mouth is best, of course."

"Specially if she's well built, huh?" The man in the blue espadrilles chortles, biting down hard on his cigar and squirting brown juice on his chin.

I walk up to Barney and whisper in his ear: "This is embarrassing." Barney slips his arm around me and draws me into the circle around the intern and his victim.

"Marry him. He'll be good to you. He's not the type that'll eat your heart out," Pinnie had said, urging me to accept Barney's pearl and sapphire engagement ring.

Barney is a good cook and an Easy Listening fan. What does it matter that I don't feel passion for him or that his jock strap hangs out of his bathing suit? Who am I to rate an Adonis? For everyone a season. Mine, I feel, is probably autumn. In the autumn of our lives, Barney and I will be a happy couple eating cilantro-seasoned omelets while listening to Easy Listening radio.

"I once had the dubious pleasure of resuscitating a corpse," the intern says.

The man in the blue espadrilles grunts.

"Well, not really an honest-to-goodness corpse in the technical sense," says the intern. *"But the man was as close to dead as any I ever saw."*

The circle narrows and the card players stop in mid-game. Barney, and I, too, are now transfixed. Mrs. Robbins curls her ponytail around her index finger, and her husband, forgetting to be a victim, sits up. The schoolteacher stops pouting and steps away from her husband's side to hear better.

"It was this very lake, in fact—a little closer to the children's crib over there," says the intern, pointing twenty yards to the right, where the guests' children are splashing around in water wings.

"It was early in the season and I'd just taken a few laps across the lake when a little guy came up to me and said, 'Guess what I just saw, Mr. Doctor!' 'What did you see, sport?' I asked him. 'I saw a black log with arms and legs floating in the water.' 'A black log with arms and legs?' 'Yes, and I think it had a face, but I couldn't tell cause it was down in the water.' I figured this kid either had a pretty surrealistic imagination or that something was wrong, so I decided to check out the 'log with the arms and legs.' The kid took me to the spot where he'd seen it, and I swam out in

that direction. I hadn't gone very far, when I bumped into something—only it wasn't a log. It was an old man. His body was bloated, his hair was full of slime, plastered to his skull, his face—"

The intern conjures the blue, waterlogged face and staring eyes of the old man, and I shudder to think that I'm fifteen years younger than Barney and may not have the opportunity to wait for happiness to come to me in the 'autumn of my life.' I recall the engagement party thrown for us by the secretaries on the seventeenth floor of Belvedere Mills, when Barney drank too much red wine and ate too much lasagna, and I held his head while he vomited in the ladies' lounge. Right after that was when I looked into Barney's bloated, waterlogged face and was sorry I'd accepted his proposal.

The intern says, "He seemed too far gone to bother with. Honestly, I was ready to push him further out, away from the shore where the kids were playing, and go back quietly for the police. But the little boy was standing there, staring at me; he just wouldn't budge. He didn't even look scared. It made me feel sort of ashamed, I guess. What do you do when a kid is watching you like that?"

"You apply first aid, that's what!" cries the man in the blue espadrilles.

"Let the man tell his story," the schoolteacher chides.

"So I dragged the body to the shore. By this time, a whole group of kids had gathered around to have a look at the 'log.' They were amazing, those kids. Didn't make a sound, didn't blink an eye. It was eerie, the way they stood there waiting to see what I would do. Believe me, I was positive the old man was finished. He had all the symptoms, no pulse, no respiration—he'd even started to turn rigid in my arms!"

Seeing that she is now lying partly in the shade, Betty-with-no-last-name gets up and pulls her chaise lounge out into the sun. After settling down on her back, she cups her silver reflector under her chin and resumes tanning her face.

"*So I started pounding the water out of him, and let me tell you there was a well inside of the old man. I mean, the water came gushing out of him like a geyser. It was a good show, a heroic effort for the kids' sake. But then it dawned on me that even if he did come to, he wouldn't be much good anyway. No oxygen in the brain for too long.*"

I grip Barney's hand and wonder if he'll become senile, and if I'll have to change his diapers and cut his hair and mince his food until he finally dies cursing me and waving a fork at me with a piece of his breakfast omelet dangling from the tines.

"*As a last resort, I decided to try mouth-to-mouth resuscitation.*"

Mitzi Dorman gasps.

"*That's exactly how I felt about it, lady,*" *says the intern.* "*What if he had some contagious disease? From the look of him, his shabby clothes, the stuff running out of him—believe me, it wasn't an appetizing thought. But it was the kids—they wouldn't leave until I had proven myself.*"

The intern steps forward, taking his listeners into his confidence. "*So I just shut my eyes, pressed my lips to his clammy mouth, and* breathed *into him.*"

The honeymooners loose a collective sigh.

"*And would you believe it, the old man started coming to?*"

"*No?*" *says Mrs. Robbins.*

"*Yessir, right there under my eyes, with me puffing and blowing myself purple in the face. The kids were suddenly jumping up and down, scaring me with the noise. Remember, it's been so quiet up till then that all you could hear was the sound of my breathing, and then the old man's feeble wheezing. But he came around.*"

"*And?*"

I think the intern is making it all up, that he and the lifeguard are playing a sick joke on the guests.

"*Well, by then the local rescue squad had arrived with all their equip-*

ment. *It's a good thing they did, because I later found out that if I'd kept it up that way I would have hyper-oxygenated the old man and done him in for lack of* CO_2."

The honeymooners nod gravely.

The intern says, "Old people can't take that much oxygen, you know."

"Did he live?" asks the man in the blue espadrilles.

"Oh, yes. I went to see him at the local hospital. They had this Indian resident on duty there—an Indian from India, I mean. It was some feat getting any information from him; his English was so hard to understand. We communicated mostly in sign language. It was ironic, the whole thing."

"Was he brain-damaged?" Mitzi Dorman calls out from the flagstone patio.

"It wouldn't have mattered either way," the intern says. "He was an escaped mental patient from the nearby State Hospital—a chronic schizophrenic, twenty-nine years in the back ward, a burnt-out case. Maybe I hadn't done him such a favor. Maybe I interfered with his one golden opportunity to finish it all—peacefully. He was still in the black hospital pajamas when I got to him. They said he wandered away from the nurse's aide when they were out walking, that he was always wandering. A peaceful type guy, not at all violent."

"But he lived?" Mitzi Dorman persists.

"Yes, if you want to call that living. And he had T.B., to add to the bargain. I had to be tested and X-rayed for a full year afterward."

The honeymooners flood the intern with admiration for his loyalty to the Hippocratic Oath and for his sacrifice. They are glad to hear of his bravery secondhand. They're glad also not to be an old man in black hospital pajamas with a tendency to wander. They are a little peeved at the unappetizing details of the story so soon before lunch, and they look at the lake as if they'll think twice before diving in. Everyone but Betty-with-

no-last-name, who has fallen asleep under her silver sun reflector and is snoring, is impressed with the intern for outwitting death. I'm certain that, unappetizing as it is, the intern's story will monopolize the dinner conversation. The guests will talk of nothing else.

I look at the intern pawing the grass with his foot and know he hasn't made up the story. I gaze at the lake where the old man had been lying face down in the black water, knowing that I will dream about the Indian, the blur of trees, the black log with arms and legs, and the curly-headed, gaping children. I know, too, that I will go on secretly despising my husband and will spend my life making it up to him.

* * *

SHARON'S WAKING DREAM ENDED, not because she wanted it to, but because her mind had gotten stuck and refused to go further. It was all vaguely connected somehow with a nagging as yet unformed image that refused to come to the surface of her thoughts. Lately, a hint of the image would turn up during her morning meditation, and she could almost catch hold of it, but just as quickly, it would disappear again. Sharon looked at the wall clock. She'd spent four hours in the library. Gathering her notes together in a neat pile, she happened to look across the table and noticed that someone had taken a seat there while she'd been engaged in her waking dream—an Indian swami in saffron robes intently reading a book on trees. Instantly, the missing image surfaced, and Sharon saw herself lying next to Rabbi Joachim in a field of clover. Both of them were naked.

THIRTEEN

THAT NIGHT, AFTER TELLING THE CHILDREN a story and tucking them in their beds herself, Sharon sat with Pinnie at the kitchen table talking peaceably and sipping tea Russian-style, as they had when Sharon's grandmother was alive and had led them in the tea drinking ritual: glasses filled almost to the brim with hot amber liquid, a steamy dividing line between the hot part of the glass and the one inch that could be comfortably held between thumb and forefinger; and raspberry jam, of course, tamped to the bottom of the glass with the back of a spoon, so much sweet raspberry jam that the glass was fairly choked with it. Berry remnants swam in amber as mother and daughter talked—idly at first—of the children, of moving to the country some day, of getting away from Brooklyn for good. Dreaming in tandem with her mother made Sharon feel pleasantly safe. Pinnie's lively good humor, her occasional curse word and uninhibited guffaw broke into the sickroom of Sharon's obsessions unrolling the blinds and throwing open the windows, announcing to the invalid that she'd taken a turn for the better—if only temporarily.

During a lull in the conversation, they listened to the ticking of the three-legged clock on the refrigerator. It had sat there for as far back as Sharon could remember. When Pinnie had moved in with Sharon she'd brought the old clock with her, creating the illusion of home. And if Paulie had not called out crazily in his sleep in Hebrew, *"Sheket babayit!"*—Quiet in the house!—and the two women had not laughed at the intrusion, might they not really have been sitting at the old kitchen table drinking tea together on a Monday night as if twenty years hadn't passed?

"That clock..." Pinnie said, looking wistfully at the ugly face with its oversized, radium-painted numbers, "I'll never throw it out. It was the first piece of 'furniture' your father and I bought when we were married."

"And the radio? Isn't it time you got a new one, that gothic church thing over there went out after World War Two."

"Why give it away, it's still good. Better than the modern one you and Arleen bought me, the alarm radio doohickey." Pinnie tossed her head and made a mock disgusted face. "Static and noise, and it only gets the all-news station anyway. Who needs news all day long? It can drive you crazy, this world."

Sharon smiled. It was comforting sitting next to her mother, their body heat mingling in the kitchen. Outside, beyond the open window, the full moon was shining on the porch and their neighbor's aging bulldog was barking asthmatically. Pinnie had set aside her glass of tea and brought her manicure tray to the table. Sharon sat with one hand soaking in the bowl of pleasantly tepid scented water while her mother coated and rubbed the other with Lady Jergens pink and creamy lotion. Pinnie knew about pressure points, and when she applied them—especially in the soft fleshy skin behind the thumb— it was like having your whole body massaged. Pinnie had wonderful hands, rough, blunt-nailed, horny with work and creeping arthritis, miraculous healing hands that had kneaded Sharon's aching shoulders with warm alcohol and Vicks Vapo-Rub and Ben-Gay, and every other foul smelling liniment when she was sick or aching after dreaded gym classes or had nearly drowned at the local Y—where every weekday afternoon she had desperately and unsuccessfully tried to learn to swim.

"Stop making mouths," Sharon said, unconsciously lapsing into her grandmother's un-translatable Yiddish expression for "Don't distort your face."

Ignoring her, Pinnie went right on distorting her face and rubbing Lady Jergens lotion into Sharon's hands. She had worked briefly in a beauty salon and was marveling just then at how little one forgets in one's lifetime. The body seemed to fall into the old grooves without even trying. Ach, a worn record of daily habits, she thought, all the way to the grave. Still, she could not help smiling as she admired her own professional manicurist's stroke.

"You know you're still pretty, Pinnie," said Sharon, "a little on the fat side, but still pretty."

Pinnie pretended to hit her. "I'll give you fat!" she laughed, flapping her hands in the air.

Sharon pretended to duck the blows, her vigorous movements causing soapy water to slosh over the sides of the bowl onto the table, the wall, and one side of the refrigerator.

"Don't get soapsuds in my tea," Pinnie said, lifting her glass with one hand and kneading Sharon's wrist with the other.

"Mmm, the glass is slippery," Sharon removed her hand from the water, making an awkward attempt to set aside her own glass of tea. Pinnie clucked her tongue and moved Sharon's glass for her. She didn't have Pinnie's deftness, tended to drop things—jars, knives. She was accident-prone, too, catching her fingers in doors and electric can openers. She never cleaned house without injuring herself and was continuously afflicted by paper cuts at work.

"Remember when you were a kid and told me you wanted to be a rich lady in a mansion with a maid? You always had your nose in a book, so I didn't make you help me around the house. I made you lazy. It's my fault; I take the blame."

Sharon put her hand back into the bowl of soapy water.

"So, who's this Italian boy you brought home the other night?" Without looking up, Pinnie continued massaging Sharon's other hand.

"He's a friend from court, from my case—now don't start," Sharon threatened to remove her hand from her mother's grasp.

"Easy, you'll spill the water," Pinnie warned, now feinting, now parrying carefully around what she had privately come to consider the "*Italian situation.*"

"The water's cold, and so is the tea," Sharon said in her mother-terrorizing tone of voice.

"I am not looking to creep into your heart, Sharon."

"Then stop creeping," Sharon snapped.

"When was it that you turned so mean? Been taking lessons maybe from your sister, the artist?"

"Please, Ma, let's not have another one of those—"

"Listen, if you think it's his religion that bothers me, you're one hundred percent wrong. It's the age difference. Yetta Solow was only five years older than Harvey and don't you think the minute she didn't watch herself and put on a pound here and a pound there he wasn't out roaming around?"

"Yeah, yeah, yeah..."

Pinnie went on, "Who knows, maybe your generation *is* different, like Arleen keeps telling me—that is, if and when she decides to talk to me. Hippies, drug addicts, women with purple hair and tattoos—who understands these things anymore? I have daughters? Snakes that spit poison in my face when I try to give them a little—"

"Enough, enough!" Sharon pulled one hand out of the water and the other away from her mother. "And you wonder why Arleen doesn't want to talk to you. "

"No respect anymore, not even to a mother. Never mind 'not even,' *especially* not to a mother." Pinnie stood up and emptied the soapy bowl of water in the sink. A pile of late-night supper dishes was drying in the rack; the ugly clock ticked its way ten-ward.

Sharon had to force herself to stay awake, listening to Pinnie's onslaught while sleeping with her eyes open—a trick she'd developed as a child knowing that her mother had high blood pressure and wasn't supposed to get excited. Feeling the old childhood guilt creep up on her, she watched Pinnie unscrew the cap of the orange medicine bottle on the shelf over the sink with trembling hands and pop a pill in her mouth. She was close to seventy now, getting older by the day. What if Pinnie were to die tonight? A moment of panic ensued. Sharon didn't want to think about that—no matter how problematic her mother was the idea of losing her was worse. She would think only positive thoughts and push aside the morbid ones. How? By using one of Rabbi Joachim's "de-stressing exercises." She half-heartedly tried visualizing Pinnie's criticism as words being tossed into the ocean and swallowed up letter by letter. No, maybe it would be better to stave off the guilt by tuning in on her mother's ramblings for a change.

"You'd say I was crazy to listen to her the way I did in those days," Pinnie was murmuring to herself. "Your grandmother was some force in all our lives, not one of us ever dared to question her. *Nobody* dared to question parents in my time. A good slap in the face I got from my stepfather when he came home from work and caught me trying on my mother's high-heeled shoes. Those were only the small things, too. You know we were four kids, four of us—and the brother, he was king because he was the only boy. He got everything without even lifting a finger. That's the way the old folks did things in those days. Boys were kings and girls were born to serve them. Me and my sisters went to work at age sixteen! That's right; we didn't even get to finish high school." Pinnie's eyes glistened with unspilled tears. Forgetting to dry the bowl, she tossed it back into the cupboard while it was still wet, closed the door with a clatter, and sat down again at the table.

She is, in spite of her coarseness, a disciplined woman, Sharon thought. Not like me.

"I had an Italian boyfriend once," Pinnie blurted out suddenly after a long pause. "My 'first love,'" she emphasized the words mockingly. "And Mama took care of that one fast enough. You remember how religious she was? She worked plenty fast on that first love of mine—none of this sitting together at the table, all palsy-walsy and pussyfooting around. You know what she did, your grandmother?"

Sharon shook her head.

"Well, I worked in a bank then; that was where I met him. I was eighteen, he was twenty-four. No, Mama didn't believe in any psychology, 'shmycology'—Mama didn't read Freud or listen to Dr. Alexander on the radio. She just marched into that bank one afternoon with a bottle of rat poison in her fist, went right up to Tony's window—he was a teller in the foreign money department—and threatened to drink down the whole bottle in front of his eyes if he kept on seeing me." Pinnie tapped herself lightly on the forehead with her finger. "Do you think it even entered my mind to question her? To tell her off? My mother's word was law. Not even a peep did she hear from me. Do you think I even so much as challenged my older sister, who I knew, as God is my witness, was the very same person who told Mama about Tony behind my back? My sister Martha? Nothing!" Pinnie smacked the table with her open palm. "I just quit my job, turned around, walked out of the bank, and never laid eyes on Tony again."

"But—"

"And don't think my heart wasn't breaking into pieces every minute. But Mama's word was law, I tell you."

"Grandma was a monster, and I never knew it," Sharon said bitterly.

"You shut up with that disrespectful talk."

Enraged, Sharon narrowed her eyes and spat out, "Maybe you ought to get yourself over to the market and buy yourself some rat poison then, because Junior Cantana has invited me to spend the weekend with him in Pennsylvania and I'm going!"

"What does your rabbi with the big black hat and the crazy eyes have to say to *that*, may I ask?" Pinnie replied sarcastically, her face flushed and her hands trembling.

"You may ask all you like—and it's damned rotten of you to talk to me like that. In case you forgot, next week is my birthday—I'll be thirty-five!" Sharon yelled, forgetting about Pinnie's blood pressure rising at the mention of Rabbi Joachim.

"All the more reason you should know better. This Junior Cantana, a boy you picked up on a bench in Coney Island, and that other one, a married man, a rabbi, no less! Feh! It's disgusting the way you've been carrying on lately."

"He's twenty-eight, will you stop calling him a *boy*? I'm going to Pennsylvania with him next weekend, to an inn. And I'll share his room—and his *bed*—if I feel like it."

"Go! Go to hell if you feel like it!"

Sharon jumped up from her chair, pushed it away from the table, and stormed out of the kitchen. Pinnie ran after her but could not catch up. By the time she reached the bedroom, Sharon had slammed the door in her mother's face. Suddenly remembering the still-wet bowl in the cupboard, Pinnie returned to the kitchen and removed it. Staring vacantly at the clock on the refrigerator, she stood rubbing the bowl with a dishtowel until her prickling fingers reminded her to stop.

Sharon, meanwhile, had dropped into bed and fallen asleep without bothering to take off her clothes. In her dream, the staircase leading to her office at the Center for Mystical Judaism was covered from top to bottom with wet green horse droppings left by a blue-faced Officer Pols sitting stiffly on his chestnut policeman's mount in the entranceway. Standing on the staircase knee-deep in horseshit, Sharon was waving at him, trying to get his attention. But Officer Pols didn't recognize her. Scowling at the mess on the stairs, he turned the horse around and galloped off in the opposite direction.

FOURTEEN

*F*ALL COMES EARLY TO THE PENNSYLVANIA *country-side this year. In mid-July, the leaves stiffen on the trees and applaud themselves in the wind. Nuts and hard sour apples fall to the roadways with a smack and split in two. Preparing for the cold, an industrious squirrel carries off the remains of an apple, quarreling noisily with her rivals as she hurries to eat the meatiest parts. Stout, buff-colored mourning doves, novice aviators rehearsing for their first foul weather flight, climb into the air after an awkward running start, gaining altitude with much laborious churning of wings. A groundhog, very brown and very fat, scuttles for cover at the approach of a passing car and dives headlong into a mound of dried leaves. The summer's languor departs quickly here; although the animals, who would have it otherwise, attempt to prolong the season—some even going so far as to ignore its passing. But the trees and meadows and woodland riding trails concede early, announcing their surrender to autumn in blinding yellow and orange before quickly turning brown and balding. This is a place where* *red worms slither out after a rainstorm, and where the sky shimmers in phosphorescent violets and oranges before sunset.*

And there is death here too, furry road kill, Sharon thought as she and Junior drove through the countryside in his borrowed Volkswagen Beetle. Reminded by the sight and smell of a flattened skunk in the road, she was still agonizing over the suicide of Jorge Diaz, which, as she'd learned earlier that morning, was the reason for the judge's final dismissal of the case against him. Was it her fault for letting Officer Pols convince her to bring the case to court in the first place? Waiting for her in the car in front of the courthouse in his gray pants, navy blue blazer, white pullover, and white moccasins, Junior looked so young and full of life that Sharon didn't have the heart to tell him that Jorge Diaz hadn't shown up for trial because he'd hung himself in his cell the night before. Not wanting to bring death into their weekend together, she'd made a stupid comment about Junior's outfit instead.

"Not a sparrow falls that God doesn't see." Now she was sitting next to Junior mentally quoting Rabbi Joachim to herself, biting into the loose raw skin of the blister on her ring finger that had begun to heal. She was wondering what kind of God let nineteen-year-old boys get hooked on drugs and hang themselves or stood by, as animals were carelessly smashed by passing cars, their moist red guts scattered across leaf-dappled roads.

It had been a pleasant drive, with almost no traffic, a Bob Dylan tape playing, and little conversation. Suddenly, as if reading her thoughts, Junior had turned down the volume and asked, "You didn't tell me what happened in court. Did Jorge show?"

"He's still confounding the lawyers." Sharon hoped her indirect answer would prevent further questions. "Now the Civil Liberties people are in it too. What a mess," she added, avoiding Junior's eyes.

"So Jorge Diaz still manages to hold up the works? I knew he'd never show up. I guess I can't blame him. Knowing what I do about the justice system now, I'd probably do the same."

Sharon shuddered. "No, you wouldn't."

On the Pennsylvania Turnpike, at the Willow Grove exit, they met a camouflaged-convoy of army vehicles traveling in the opposite direction with their lights on. Sharon counted ten in all. Junior held up two fingers in a V, exchanging peace signs with the driver of the first truck.

"When we first met, I thought you were a rightwing military fanatic," Sharon said.

"And now what do you think I am?"

"Oh, a lefty peacenik."

"Are you sorry you met me?" Junior gave her a brief but meaningful glance.

"Do you want me to say 'no'—because I'm happy now, because I'm delighted to have met you, and because, though you still know so little about me, really, you're about to take me to bed with you?"

Junior nodded, grinning. "I'm a patient type of guy."

"Okay, no, I'm not sorry I met you," Sharon said, turning her face to him.

"Good, neither am I," Junior said, and stroked her cheek.

The plan was to pick up Junior's friends Icaro, an army doctor, and his wife Wendy, an army nurse, at the Veterans' Hospital in Valley Forge. The four of them would picnic in the State Park and then drive to the Purple Hen Inn in Buck's County, where Junior had made dinner reservations and booked a room for the night. He'd enthusiastically described it to her as they neared Valley Forge: the big four-poster bed with its goose-down quilt and crisp, crackly white linens, the country wallpaper patterned with rose-bowered cottages set amid gently rising slopes of a valley. The wallpaper would be ever so slightly faded, but charming, and the varnished wooden floorboards would be cool under your naked toes. There would be a rocker in the corner by the window, a bowed weeping willow outside, and a view of the lazy Delaware Canal from a balcony so narrow it could only hold one person at a time. The bathroom would be spotless, with an old-fashioned, clawfoot tub...

Their car passed through the hospital gates, and Junior pointed out the Officer's Club, the Commissary and the PX. The M.P. at the gate brusquely demanded to see his pass, and Junior, annoyed, but smiling, opened his wallet and flashed his ID. Sharon imagined what Rabbi Joachim would have done in the same situation and almost burst out laughing at how, ignoring the sentry, he'd have floored the gas pedal and barreled his red Volvo right past the gate.

With its shaded walks and flower gardens, the hospital resembled a college campus except that the patients wandering aimlessly across the grounds were wearing slippers and striped bathrobes, the heavily medicated ones ashen-faced and stupefied. Most were hopelessly young, jug-eared, and soft-skinned. Sharon's heart clenched.

"Why are some patients wearing black pajamas?" she asked after Junior had parked the car in a space marked *Military Personnel Only* and they were walking toward the main building.

"They have T.B. It's to distinguish them from the others. You know, I never thought about it before."

"What did you wear when you were here?"

"Me? When I was well enough, I wore civvies and worked."

"You worked? A patient recovering from a battle wound?" Sharon asked incredulously.

"Yeah, it was part of my rehab. The docs didn't think it would be a good idea for me to sit around, so they had me painting signs in the workshop. I'm an artist, so they figured I'd want to paint something."

"Oh, yes—army logic, right?"

Junior pushed open the heavy front door and waited for Sharon to step into a corridor smelling heavily of disinfectant. Lowering her eyes so as not to stare at the maimed, limbless, bandaged, and wheelchair-bound men in the corridor, she took his hand. But it was impossible not to look at the wounded men. Like Jorge Diaz, they would haunt her dreams—today, tomorrow, forever. It was cruel of Junior to bring her inside. Why didn't he let her wait in the car? Sharon was about to tell him this when a small, dark man with a handle-bar mustache wearing a white coat with a stethoscope sticking out of the pocket rushed at Junior from the other end of the corridor and gave him a hug. Under the white coat he was wearing a mustard-colored corduroy jacket, a blue denim shirt, and a rumpled pair of chinos; a woman in riding boots carrying a small fluffy white dog in her arms was following close behind him.

"Icaro Lagan, Wendy Lagan, this is Sharon Berg."

"Sharon?" Icaro pronounced the "r" with a rolling trill, inevitably bringing Rabbi Joachim to mind. Unlike the rabbi, however, Icaro shook her hand warmly and looked her in the eye as he did so.

"Wendy..."

"Nice to meet you. And this is Allie," Wendy said, holding out the dog for Sharon to pet.

So this woman in the oversized, gray flannel sweatshirt with the hole in the shoulder and the faded jeans owned the Beetle. As always, Sharon had overdressed for the occasion. Even in her stylish flat-heeled ballerina slippers (so as not to look too much taller than Junior), her stockings and full city regalia—handbag, crocheted summer gloves, scarf and earrings—it was Sharon who came off looking awkward. Despite Wendy's shabby outfit, she was too pretty to compete with. Sharon excused herself and headed for her usual refuge—the toilet. Once inside the tiny white cubbyhole with the lidless toilet seat and the patch-in-the-wall window, she washed her hands and face and dried them with a rough paper towel from a pile on the sink. Finding no wastebasket, she dropped the crumpled towel into the toilet bowl, flushed it down, and, pulling up her wrinkled panty hose from the waistband, checked her face in the mirror: rouged cheeks made even redder by the towel rub; blue eyes glistening with unnatural ardor for a twenty-eight-year-old goy who, in approximately seven hours, would be mounting her. Hearing voices outside the door, Sharon took a deep breath before leaving the toilet.

On emerging, she heard Wendy breathlessly explaining to Junior that she'd rushed right to the hospital from her riding lesson, where she'd lost a stirrup and landed flat on her rump in the dust, and had had no time to go home and change her clothes. Watching her as she talked, Sharon anxiously noted that Wendy wasn't just pretty but *beautiful*, small and delicately boned with green eyes and thick red-gold hair that she wore plaited over her ears into a low bun tucked behind her graceful flower stalk of a neck.

Icaro laughed and patted his wife's head consolingly. It didn't seem to bother him that he was over forty and Wendy was only in her twenties. The age difference between them was greater than that between Sharon and Junior. But Icaro was a man—and a doctor to boot. Junior had only introduced her as Sharon Berg. What else had he told his friends about her? That she was a secretary? A Kabbalah student?

"Icaro taught me Spanish," Wendy said, handing her husband the dog before turning to a wall locker behind her and removing a gallon-sized cooler. "And I taught him English. We both did so well at it that we decided to prolong the language course and get married."

"Don't believe her," said Icaro, putting the leash on the dog. He removed his white coat and handed it to Wendy, who stored it in the locker. "I only married her for her body. You know these legendary, sexy American nurses." Somehow, coming from Icaro, with his rolled "r" and his laughable handlebar mustache, the remark didn't come across as sexist.

"Here, I'll get it," Junior took the cooler.

"I like your dog," Sharon said, edging closer to Wendy, who, in the brief span of their meeting, had elicited an unpleasant childhood recollection also involving a dog. Wendy was now provoking the same turbulent mixture of rage and desire to maim her perfect beauty.

"What's your doggie's name?" Sharon had asked upon meeting the little girl walking her dog on a late winter afternoon. Dressed all in pink, amazed that the older girl had deigned to talk to her, the child had shaken her long red curls under her peaked cap and submissively, or out of friendliness—Sharon was not sure which—handed her the dog's leash.

"His name's Fluffy. Here, you wanna walk him for a while?"

They'd walked on together, Sharon holding the dog's leash in one hand and the child's mittened hand in the other.

"Your mommy lets you walk the dog alone so late?"

"Just today; Toby went to her Girl Scout meeting and Mommy has company, so there was nobody home to do it but me."

They had neared the subway station then and were approaching a little hole-in-the-wall candy store, a favorite with the neighborhood children for its gargantuan comic book displays, its long zinc soda bar, and its nearsighted, easygoing proprietor, Mr. Fort, who'd let them read the comic books without buying and occasionally handed out free pencil holders at the beginning of the school year.

"Do you like Pickup Sticks?" Overwhelmed by an unfamiliar tide of generosity, Sharon had wanted to buy something for the child.

The little girl had been puzzled but let herself be led into the store.

On credit, for she had no money with her, Sharon had bought a long tube of blue and yellow magnetic Pickup Sticks—the most expensive kind—and given it to the little girl.

"*Thank you,*" *the trusting child had again taken her hand and walked with her out of the candy store.*

"*Let's go to my house and try them out.*" *Gripped by an impulse that brought fear to her stomach and bile to her throat, Sharon hadn't waited for an answer but had gone home with both child and dog in tow.*

The Kellners were then living in the Midwood section of Brooklyn in a small red brick, two-family house whose front hall door was hung with curtains and could be locked from the inside. Pinnie was working as a manicurist in a beauty salon on Flatbush Avenue. Her father, Sharon thought, might be with his "woman," the black-haired creature she heard her parents arguing over at night when she was supposed to be sleeping. Breathing heavily, she'd slung the dog's leash over the doorknob after locking the door, tossed off her parka and removed the little girl's coat.

"*Let's stay here, it's cozier, don't you think?*" *she said, sitting down with the child and the dog on the living room floor. Opening the tube, she tossed the Pickup Sticks onto the carpet. The radiator hissed, and the child, now openly frightened, began to whimper.*

"*Oh, don't be such a fraidy cat,*" *Sharon said, placing her cold hand against the girl's warm neck under her silky red curls.*

"*I want to go home! I want my mommy!*"

The dog now began to howl so loud that Sharon had to cover her ears. It was a crazy, stupid thing to have done, bringing the girl home, and when people heard about it—for surely the little girl would hurry off first thing and blab to her mother and her sister Toby about it—and the child's mother might choose to press charges and have Sharon expelled from school or even worse, placed in juvenile detention. Her friends would throw her out of their club for molesting Toby's little sister and titter behind their hands as she walked past them on her way to see her counselor. She'd be friendless and alone forever. Her father would be so ashamed of her that he'd never so much as look at her again. Enraged as

*the enormity of her as yet uncommitted crime loomed before her in the
lengthening evening shadows beyond the curtained door, Sharon joined
the howling dog and the child and began to cry, too. "Damn you, damn
you!" she screamed at the little girl, who had tears and snot running down
her chin. Then, roughly pulling up the little girl by the arm and quickly
slipping her back into her coat, Sharon had unwound the dog's leash,
opened the door, and sent her on her way.*

*Miraculously, no one had ever found out about it. After a while, Sha-
ron herself believed what she'd done that afternoon to be a dream or a
raging fantasy entertained at the sight of all that pinkness and innocence.*

Whatever the evil thing had been, it eventually loosened its grip
on her. She'd even forgotten it—until the brush and feel of the child-
woman Wendy colliding with her in the hospital corridor brought it
rushing back so powerfully it almost knocked her over.

"People eat dogs in Korea," Icaro was saying as they walked down
the stairs and through the Lysol-smelling corridors, once again surrounded by the army of limbless and broken men. "I saved Allie from
the casserole, you might say."

"Oh, honey, it wasn't all that dramatic; how you love to exagger-
ate." Wendy playfully slapped her husband's butt.

Spurred by the affectionate display of his friends, Junior pulled
Sharon close to him when they were seated in the back of the car. Her
heart banging against her ribs, Sharon wondered if she wasn't falling
in love with him after all.

* * *

IT WAS AN IDEAL PICNIC, RIGHT OUT OF A MOVIE. No, even
better, because Sharon was participating in it herself rather than long-
ing for it from the wrong side of a lonely late-night television screen.

Searching for a way to make it last—the shady grove of trees, their laughter melting into the wind, everything so green, so green, even the wine bottles glinting in the sun—despite Rabbi Joachim's warning against clinging to the "fugitive pleasures of the flesh"—Sharon wished she could restrain the fleeting moment, catch it in her fist and hold it forever. As the sun descended and the talk grew livelier, she even let Junior Cantana put his arm around her in full view of the Lagans—though that might have resulted from her three glasses of champagne. *You know that drinking wine with gentiles is forbidden because it might lead to intermarriage*, Rabbi Joachim's astral voice intruded. Icaro had opened another bottle of champagne. Sharon held out her glass and let him fill it to the top. All she needed was another sip, and the rabbi would stop haranguing her.

Wendy's plaid cooler was filled with random delicacies: a minuscule jar of black caviar; a variety of biscuits; a pungent wheel of orange cheese that was not cheddar but whose name escaped Wendy for the moment; organic purple grapes; brandied peaches; champagne; and a chocolate cake Wendy had baked herself. She seemed to have tossed in whatever had come to mind. Yet despite her childlike disregard for practicality, Wendy had remembered to bring plastic knives, forks, spoons and glasses, and paper plates, along with a set of richly embossed linen napkins, a wedding gift, as she put it, "from one of Icaro's diamond-studded Colombian aunts." She'd even included a Frisbee and a Scrabble set and a small cassette player.

"Icaro loves American jazz. He simply has to have blues wherever he goes. Isn't this cake delicious? I'm going to have another piece." Wendy cut herself a large slice of chocolate cake and licked her fingers.

"Watch it, or you'll get fat, like your mother, maybe. No, heaven forbid, what am I saying?" Icaro rolled his eyes in mock horror. "You should see this woman, she's an elephant!"

Wendy slapped him on the hand, spilling some of his champagne.

"*Tiene.* enough, little devil! She's impossible, my wife, but I love her anyway. You love her, too, Sharon, yes?" Icaro bent forward and peered, smiling, into Sharon's eyes. "I can tell. She is impossible, an elf, a perpetual child, but everyone love her anyway." Tipsy, Icaro forgot his English.

"Some elf," Junior said. Covering the opening with a napkin, he freed the cork from the last champagne bottle with a dull, popping noise. "That 'eternal child,' I'll have you know..."

"*Perpetual* child, I said *perpetual*," Icaro corrected him, exaggeratedly rolling his Rs.

"Okay, *perpetual*," Junior said, imitating Icaro's Latin trill and waving his napkin in the air. "That elf over there is entering medical school a month from now."

Sharon tried to imagine what was expected of her—a curtsy? What to say without betraying her envy?

Wendy leapt up from the blanket and tossed the Frisbee high in the air. "Come on, all, come join me before the sun goes down and it's too late to play!"

"I'm—I'm impressed," Sharon said finally, slipping off her shoes, and noticing a large, unsightly hole in her stocking and her big toe sticking out.

"All my inspiration, of course," Icaro said, indifferent to Sharon's predicament. "My wife is a perfectly good nurse as it is, but we plan to return to Colombia to work together. Where I intend to practice, I'll need an associate, someone who can perform surgery and prescribe her own medicines."

"They're going to work in the jungle, near the Amazon," Junior said.

"Are you playing Frisbee or not?" Accompanied by a spirited classical Spanish guitar piece on the cassette player, Wendy danced over to the blanket and aimed the Frisbee directly at the champagne bottle. The dog was furiously digging a hole alongside her.

"I'll play if it'll keep you from knocking over the champagne," Junior got up and beckoned for Wendy to toss him the Frisbee. "Anyone else?" He looked down at Sharon, clearly eager for her to join him. Sharon was too intent on hiding the offending hole in her stocking to respond, and sat busily stacking used paper plates and cups and throwing them into an oversized trash bag.

"You don't have to play," said Icaro. "Stay here and talk to me."

"Yes," Sharon said, "*you* play, Junior. I'll clean up, it's getting late." Unthinkingly slipping into her motherly role, she'd almost called him "Paulie."

Icaro was watching her closely, with a half smile on his lips. "So you are the martyr type," he said holding open the trash bag for Sharon as Junior returned Wendy's toss high over her head eliciting shrieks and mock threats of revenge.

Deliberately returning Icaro's insult with one of her own, Sharon said pettishly, "She almost looks too young for med school."

"Yes, she hides her brilliance under that playful little girl's mask—but she'll make a better doctor than I am. Intelligence was not much prized in her family—not for women, anyway. The mother is a rich widow out in Ohio—I only saw her once in my life, at the Philadelphia airport. She flew in to meet me after Wendy and I had married. The three of us had a stiff drink and a stiff conversation, and she flew right back home. She's probably disowned Wendy by now; but we haven't heard from her in a couple of years. Wendy was not supposed to have become a nurse. She was not supposed to join the army, and she certainly, so her mother thought, had no business marrying a foreigner."

"Don't you come from a wealthy family yourself?" Sharon suppressed a hiccup and noticed a sliver of moon hidden behind a scudding cloud. It would grow dark soon and a full moon the color of a new nickel would come out of hiding.

"My father is wealthy, but not me. I am a Communist," Icaro said proudly thumping himself on the chest. "You know, the Garcia Marquez variety—he's Colombian, too."

"Who?" Sharon shivered. It had turned colder now that the sun was setting. "Marquez. *One Hundred Years of Solitude.*"

Resentful of Icaro for testing her, Sharon shrugged and said, "Oh, him. I've never been a great fan of magical realism."

Ignoring the offhanded dismissal of his compatriot, Icaro leaned back and half closed his eyes. "Yes, that is my plan, to go home to Colombia, and make things better for the poor people in my country." He paused, then stood up and stuffed the remains of their beautiful picnic further into the sack in order to make room for the empty champagne bottles. Allie had stopped digging holes and was lying prone on the ground, alert and sniffing the air as if testing for rain.

From the corner of her eye, Sharon watched the light-footed Wendy scramble for the Frisbee. Junior, in the shadows now, seemed to be beckoning her. Sharon had missed the rest of Icaro's sentence. The testiness between them had dissipated and he was now telling her, very amiably, about his internship in the primitive Colombian mountain country, of surgeries performed in graveyards, of starving babies with blue noses and huge swollen bellies—painting Sharon's own worst nightmares in the bright colors of his "Communist ideals"—going on about his hopes for the future of his country, his admiration for his atypical American wife, who had been accepted by Tufts University Medical School for the coming term—despite her late application, and her being a married woman. Wasn't Wendy amazing, he asked rhetorically, not waiting for Sharon's reply. And then, before she could nod benignly and signal her agreement—yes, Wendy was fantastic, a new

Mother Teresa in the making—Icaro suddenly interrupted himself and said, "God, how I love that woman. My kindest wish for my good friend Junior is that you and he are as happy as we are after you marry."

It was surely Latino overstatement, or maybe, the champagne, or the overwhelming surge of love Icaro was feeling for his wife just then. But no, for when Sharon pretended not to hear his last remark, he continued, "You are a fine couple, you will be happy together, I know. Maybe you will even come to live and work in my country and be—how do you call it?" Icaro gazed up among the trees and twirled his fingers searching for the lost word. "Ah, yes, *neighbors*, good neighbors and friends."

"You're running ahead of yourself, Icaro. Junior and I hardly know each other. We met less than a month ago, sitting on a bench in Coney Island."

"Where is that place, somewhere in New York City?" he scowled, looking like a well-meaning gnome.

Why was this stranger with the handlebar moustache asking her these personal questions? She'd only met him and his "elfin" wife a few hours ago. They meant nothing to her.

Yapping, the dog jumped up and circled the legs of his returning mistress.

"I know for a fact that he is in love with you," Icaro went on hurriedly, as if it were important to deliver this information to her before Junior and Wendy returned. "He told me so himself. As for time, why do you think of time? Love is stronger than time," he finished sententiously, shaking the crumbs from the green army blanket and whistling for the dog to come and eat the few remaining scraps of food from his hand.

Only love is stronger than death, Rabbi Joachim whispered through the trees.

Help me, Rabbi, I am looking for the right man to love, the right life! But Sharon's plea was lost in the rustle of the leaves.

FIFTEEN

THE ROOM AT THE PURPLE HEN INN was just as Sharon had visualized it: an enormous four-poster bed; a blue-and-white porcelain pitcher and basin on a spindle-legged table; and a big window overlooking the Delaware Canal. It wasn't until she pulled aside the curtains and found herself confronted by a thick brown stream swollen with filth that she remembered Wendy's warning: "It's picturesque, but the Delaware is one of the most heavily polluted bodies of water in the country."

Sharon quickly drew the curtains, opened her overnight bag, and, after removing her cosmetics, lined them up in the bathroom medicine cabinet. Junior had gone into the Lagans' room to borrow an extra hanger, mercifully leaving her alone to remove her underwear and stuff it quickly into the top drawer of the bureau. She was in too much of a hurry to notice that her plastic diaphragm case had come loose from its hiding place in the folds of a slip—in her last-minute abandon, she'd hidden it there—and it clattered to the floor just as Junior entered the room.

Skeejit! cried a saucy blue jay perched on the windowsill, distracting him while Sharon hurriedly retrieved the case and shoved it into the drawer. She was certain he'd seen her drop it but was tactful enough not to say anything.

They took dinner on the inn's big, screened-in porch. The temperature had dropped and a chill wind blew through the trees. Sharon shivered and was about to suggest they go inside where there were several empty tables, but Wendy wouldn't hear of eating indoors on a full moon night like this, and, removing her own shawl, draped it around Sharon's shoulders.

"Don't worry, Sharon. You'll warm up after a drink or two," said Icaro, rubbing his tapered fingers together as if blessing the table. He had shaved and slicked back his hair with water. Sitting next to him, Sharon could smell his heavy, pungent cologne. The points of his handlebar moustache glimmered in the candlelight, reminding her of a circus ringmaster. All he needed was a red dress coat, a silk top hat, a pair of black boots, and a brass-headed whip.

"Waitress!" Icaro snapped his fingers. "We're ready to order now."

Some Communist, Sharon thought.

Wendy had changed into a short, sleeveless pink summer dress that revealed her bare tan legs to their best advantage. She wore midsize circular gold earrings but no makeup and was, Sharon grudgingly noted, even more beautiful without it.

Icaro ordered whiskey sours all around, and then, as the meal was brought to the table (in deference to Rabbi Joachim, Sharon had ordered filet of sole—a fish with gills being neither Kosher nor non-Kosher but somewhere in-between) and a whole carafe of Sangria was emptied and replaced by a second, Junior and Icaro regaled the women with army jokes, making them laugh almost to choking at the sheer stupidity of their commanding officers. Suddenly, Junior pointed at Sharon and, addressing the table at large, asked, "What do you think of this Kosher Jewish girl dating this Italian boy?" Sharon shrank into her seat. Fortunately, there was too much loud conversation and laughter among the heavily drinking diners on the porch and his friends didn't hear him. Spurred by the wine, Icaro launched into an Amazonian folk song with a tremolo refrain and Junior, not to be outdone, displayed the rose tattoo on his leg. Their boyish silliness ended by the time the dessert arrived, the talk moved to politics, with Icaro expounding his socialist goals for the peasants of the lower Amazon. Pounding the table with his fist, he ranted against his "parasitic" Colombian plantation-owning cousins and their CIA backers for what he called "La Violencia." The usually effervescent Wendy did not seem especially compelled to talk, and sat gazing placidly at the stagnant moonlit canal. Sharon was trying to imagine what Wendy was thinking when Junior suddenly touched her knee under the table, reminding her of what was awaiting her in the big four-poster bed upstairs.

The moon traveled across the sky. Frogs croaked in the bulrushes lining the canal; the diners were beginning to leave the restaurant and the laughter and conversation gave way to the sound of mating crickets rubbing their legs together under the porch. The temperature had dipped even further, and Sharon was not only shivering but her teeth were now chattering. Suddenly a woman at a neighboring table let out a shriek, and the manager rushed over to see what was wrong.

"It's nothing," the woman's embarrassed companion assured him. "Just a little bat. My wife's afraid of them."

"A bat!" The three waitresses serving the diners on the porch dashed behind the bar in tandem.

"What is it?" Always gallant, Icaro was already standing, poised to come to the aid of the damsels in distress.

"A bat—a bat, the horrid thing! I hate them!" the woman at the next table screamed. Her husband remained seated and waved his credit card at the waitresses hiding behind the bar. He, too, appeared to be afraid of the bat.

"They're both terrified," Wendy said quietly to Icaro. "You'd better go over there."

Sharon was now frightened as well as cold. She knew from her reading that bats did not get tangled up in people's hair and that a bat bite was dangerous only if the bat was rabid, which was rare. But this didn't stop her from being afraid.

Icaro walked across the porch to the bar where the bat had landed before ascending to the rafter immediately above it.

"That's my husband," said Wendy, "always number one on the scene."

"I'll say," Junior agreed thickly, "old 'Lifesaver Lagan' himself."

For about ten seconds no one on the porch moved.

"There aren't any bats here, it was probably just a big moth," the restaurant manager said dismissively.

Suddenly, the bat swooped down in a rapid Kamikaze arc, almost grazing the ear of the poor blue-lipped woman who had first spotted it. One of the waitresses hiding behind the bar screamed and bolted for the kitchen. Curious, or more likely too ashamed to follow her, everyone else on the porch stayed put. The excitement had drawn a crowd of diners from the indoor tables to the doorway of the porch making it difficult to leave even if anyone wanted to.

Sharon now saw the event in two ways: on the one hand, the bat—or whatever it was—which was hiding again, could have been sent to her as a warning sign from Rabbi Joachim to get up and leave the inn before she had compromised herself. Another possibility was that the rabbi had embodied himself in the form of a bat to personally prevent her intended sin of fornication.

"That's crazy altogether," Sharon said aloud. Fortunately, the others thought she was talking about the situation at hand and made no comment. The creature chose that moment to make its second dive, and in the full light of the candle on the table, was revealed in all its "batness": scalloped wings, downy marsupial fur, beady black eyes—taking into account its Transylvanian cinematic associations, of course. If indeed it was the embodied astral form of Rabbi Joachim come to save Sharon from the inevitable fornication about to take place upstairs... But she had no time to pursue that thought any further, for at that moment the bat soared upward and flew out over the canal through the same unnoticed hole in the porch screen through which it had entered.

"Die Fledermaus!" Icaro shouted, pulling Wendy up from her seat. The two of them started waltzing around the porch.

Something had definitely gone wrong. If, as Sharon now believed, the bat *was* the astral Rabbi Joachim signaling her downfall, something had gone terribly wrong. Instead of curtailing Sharon's sexual impulses, it was as if the bat's entry and dramatic exit had provided everyone on the porch a license to run wild. The uptight husband and wife at the next table were locking tongues in an openly erotic display of relief; the manager was fondling the breasts of the most buxom of the three waitresses in full view of the diners; Icaro and Wendy were no longer waltzing but rubbing up against each other; and Junior was leading Sharon through the crowd and up the stairs to their room. Yes, if she were on the other side of the screen, winging her way through the cold, spooky moonlit night alongside Rabbi Joachim, Sharon would definitely have judged the scene on the porch the result of a Kabbalistic formula gone terribly awry.

* * *

REFLECTED IN THE BATHROOM MIRROR ON THE DOOR, Sharon surveyed her naked body while Junior lay on the bed waiting for her. How long ago was it that she'd dropped her diaphragm case on the floor? And here she was, holding it again in her hands, not daring to open it just yet. Still, Rabbi Joachim pleaded with her: *There's still time, Sharon. You don't have to do this.*

At first they had kept their clothes on as they were lying side by side on top of the eiderdown quilt, but then, despite her protests, Junior had insisted on showing her the long pink scar left by the wound on his belly, and taken off his shirt. Sharon had expected the scar to be worse and said she was relieved to see that it had healed so well. To keep from running her finger across the scar, she'd asked him exactly how he'd gotten the wound, and Junior had described the ride in the jeep with the soldier who'd been blown up beside him right after handing him the skull on the chain for good luck. Sharon stared at the ashtray on the night table with "Colonial Inn, Sarasota, Fla." inscribed around the rim in big black letters and wondered what an ashtray from Florida was doing in the non-smoking room of an inn in New Hope, Pennsylvania. Finally unable to restrain herself, she'd touched Junior's smooth, taut, scarred stomach and, moving down to kiss it, let her face be smothered in the piney sweetness of his flesh.

A landmine had exploded directly under the jeep Junior was in. Junior believed he'd been saved by his friend's skull charm, ordered from one of those ads on the back of a pumping iron magazine. He'd been so sure of it that he'd broken down, refused to talk to anyone, refused to accept the medal his C.O. had pressed into his clenched fist as he lay recuperating from his gut wound. He hated the army. He hated himself for surviving when there was nothing left of his friend to be put in a box and sent home.

Sitting up, Sharon continued stroking Junior's stomach.

"Icaro said it was the guilt over my buddy's death that set me off, the idea that there was some kind of magic attached to that skull, and that in taking it from him, I'd taken his life. But that's all over now. Being with Icaro and Wendy these past few months has taught me that the only magic in life is what you make of it yourself."

"Icaro is a born debunker."

"He's a doctor, not a medicine man."

"Yes, but they're related," Sharon said, hearing faint music from behind the thin wall separating them from the Lagans. Was it Frank Sinatra singing "Embraceable You"? She couldn't tell; the volume was turned down too low.

"Of course magic doesn't fit into Icaro's life scheme, he's a Communist. He and Wendy have everything so perfectly tallied up. It makes you sort of hate them a little, doesn't it?"

"Poor Sharon," said Junior, unexpectedly placing his hand on her breast, then moving it down to caress her belly, hips, and thighs.

I need him now, but I don't love him, Sharon thought.

Letting him explore her body with his hands, she said, "Did you ever wonder why such a cold, sterile, and airless lump like the moon would be associated with love?"

"Take off your clothes," he answered, his voice low, almost menacing, as he tugged at her skirt.

And that's what had brought her into the bathroom where she now stood, surveying her small, goose-bumped breasts and taut red nipples in the mirror. Her aroused nipples appeared to be staring back at her. Sharon turned around and inspected the skin on her back for pimples. The awkward bas relief of her naked spine stood out like a bony ruin on an empty plain. She could delay the inevitable no longer. She removed the diaphragm from its case, smeared it with KY Jelly, and deftly inserted it. Turning off the bathroom light behind her and covering her pudenda with both hands like the modest Jewish virgin she wasn't, she tiptoed across the cold bedroom floor and joined Junior in bed.

In the next room, Wendy had turned up the volume on the tape recorder. She and Icaro were probably dancing naked. The dog that he'd rescued from the strangely ravenous Koreans was probably lying on its back near Wendy's riding boots, dreaming of bones, and hitching its legs in the air.

Sharon heard the music clearly now. "Embrace me, my sweet embraceable you." It *was* Frank Sinatra. Another Italian, like the one hovering over her, the red eyes in the sockets of the mournful skull on the chain around his neck twinkling lugubriously in the dark. Her body taut as a tightrope, strung between panic and laughter, she'd forgotten to ask Junior if he was wearing a condom. She hadn't thought to look. But it was too late. Junior had entered her by then, and the tightrope split in two. Unbidden, like the sudden stab of pain he was inflicting on her, came the stomach-wrenching image of Jorge Diaz hanging in his cell: bulging eyes, head lolling off to one side, saliva-streaked chin and semen-stained pajamas. No matter how hard she tried, Sharon could not get that hideous face to go away. It grew bigger and bigger as Junior pumped and heaved and groaned, thrusting inside of her, and though she fought like mad to allow herself to enjoy the pleasure she was feeling, the stars bursting forth new worlds throughout her body in an orgasm like no other she'd ever experienced before, she felt nothing but disgust even as Junior emptied himself and their lovemaking ended. When he withdrew, she was relieved to see that he'd been wearing a condom.

Sharon turned uncomfortably in the oversized bed and half sat up, resting on her elbow. Junior Cantana lay beside her, spent, his shoulder blocking a clear view of his face.

"Are you circumcised?" It was a stupid, inappropriate thing to say, but it was all she could think of at the moment.

"A lot of guys my age were circumcised at birth, Jewish or not. It was considered healthy. So, yes, I'm circumcised."

"I'm sorry for asking," Sharon said, ashamed. She hadn't been at all responsive lying there rigidly, letting him do all the work; now he must be musing on her failure to respond—thinking it was because she'd feared that he wasn't circumcised. Or maybe he was disappointed because he'd heard somewhere that older women were better in bed because they were hornier, or maybe he loved her and thought the sex had been great. He was probably thinking that she must have wanted him badly enough to have come this far.

To make up for her poor performance, Sharon wanted to say something nice but couldn't—later, maybe tomorrow morning when they were driving home together. She'd insist on leaving earlier than planned; she couldn't stay here another day. She would explain to him then, in the car, how the sudden startling image of Jorge's face had merged with his as he'd hovered over her, his death's head pendant sweeping back and forth in front of her; how the face kept changing so fast—three times in succession—from Jorge Diaz to that of a dying old man with a foam-flecked mouth until it had been transformed into facelessness, leaving nothing behind but a black, headless log bobbing up and down in the darkness. What she would not tell him was that there had been yet another face, the final one—that of Rabbi Joachim. And that it was still there, hovering in front of her, even with her eyes open.

Junior had fallen asleep and was snoring softly. Sharon looked over at the radio clock on the night table and saw that it was past midnight. She would tell him tomorrow, too, that she'd been ashamed for having let him bring her here and letting him fuck her as if she were some alley cat in heat, that she resented him for luring her into it with the aphrodisiac of his pine-scented body.

Tomorrow, in Wendy's Volkswagen, she would tell him, finally, about her love for Rabbi Joachim, whom she could never leave—not for any man—and she would break it off with Junior Cantana once and for all.

SIXTEEN

THERE WAS A COMMOTION IN THE BASEMENT of
Priceman's Occult Books. It was only ten-thirty on a Tuesday
morning, an otherwise slow day because of the cloudburst
that had turned into a full-fledged rainstorm, when Seymour's sallow-
faced nephew, always on the alert, had thought to turn the "Open"
sign around to read "Closed: *Cerrado* Until Noon." Only a handful
of customers browsed upstairs, two whose faces Priceman's nephew
didn't recognize, and a lady aura reader in a blue Salvation Army-
style suit wearing a neck brace, waving at him with her booklist from
the other end of the store. If she were not such a good customer, he
might have ignored her, for it was a true effort for Priceman's nephew
to smile—evenly half-heartedly, as he was now. Secretly, well, not so
secretly (for every so often he was known to air his views aloud) he had
no use for the "kooks" who were always hanging around, sniffing his
benevolent (read: "sucker") Uncle Seymour's ankles like dogs around a
fire hydrant. Take this one, for example, Priceman's nephew muttered,
as he flipped the blue-and-white sign on the door, hoping the aura

reader with the punch-drunk boxer's nose and gooey eyes would take the cue and leave. Given the fact that her unpaid credit was three stapled pages long, you'd have thought Seymour would have gotten rid of her long ago. Not a chance. Not only did Seymour let her pay off her bills on a nonexistent "layaway plan"—he didn't even add a monthly finance charge. As if that weren't enough, on her mammoth-sized mail orders, his sucker uncle omitted the cost of shipping and handling!

"She's a sick woman, an old maid with no one and nothing but aura reading to live for," Seymour would say by way of justification for his largesse, hunching his rounded shoulders, licking the tape, and sealing and addressing the package himself. "She can't even turn her neck to see who's behind her. I just hope she doesn't get mugged one of these days."

Not contented with her special privileges, the aura reader would corner the nephew and besiege him with stories of psychic experiences from her childhood in Lincoln, Massachusetts—during inventory, no less, when he was busiest. Brandishing a thick sheaf of booklists she'd clipped out of theosophical magazine indexes and pasted on long yellow sheets of legal paper, she would then turn the subject (insidiously, like all religious fanatics, he thought) to the Search for God Society or the Association for Edgar Cayce Research in the frail but persistent hope that he might join in. The nephew was single—a skinny, confirmed bachelor who shared his dingy Upper West Side hotel room with a cat, two withered palm plants, and a radio. He had no intention of marrying, had never dated when his parents were alive and saw no reason to start doing so after they died. It therefore never occurred to him that the aura reader's probing into his religious life might be a lonely spinster's way of asking him to dinner.

For her part, the aura reader was never sure of the nephew's reasons for avoiding her. She thought he might be shy. But the smile he returned to her today was so sour that she quickly charged her books at the cash register and left without pressing on him her usual lists. She was the last to leave; the store was now empty of customers. Outside, in the bleak downtown streets, the rain fell in thick sheets against the dusty storefront. Good that it's raining, the nephew thought, at least it saves us the cost of a window washer this week. He signaled the stringy-haired girl at the counter to let no one into the store until otherwise informed before returning, his lip curled in disdain, to the scandal downstairs. His doctor, only two weeks ago, had warned him of ulcers if he continued to torture himself over the business, so the nephew made a conscious effort to remain calm and to take the stairs slowly. He even paused to glance at a bright orange notice with black lettering announcing the arrival of a new Indian Messiah at Hunter College in September. Not in my lifetime, thought the non-believer, as he caught the first loud shouts coming from Seymour's basement cubicle. Then, straightening his skinny woolen tie over his protruding Adam's apple, he descended.

Priceman's inner sanctum, the cubicle of cubicles, was an exact square, running ten feet by ten feet either way. The walls were lined with books culled from esoteric libraries all over the world: wrinkled yellow volumes from Philo to Zoroaster; an eighteenth-century leather bound edition of the *Malleus Maleficarum,* worth fifteen hundred dollars; three Sanskrit versions of *The Lotus of the True Law*; and Rabbi Joachim's own seven-volume translation of the Zohar shared a special glass-enclosed hutch reserved for Seymour's personal collection of "the rarest of the rare." The floor was partially covered by two skimpy, foot-worn Hamadan carpets thrown catty-corner to each other at a time when Mrs. Priceman had thought to undertake the decorating of her husband's private office. Unfortunately, she'd gotten into an argument with one of the Priceman daughter-in-laws, a heavy-cheeked young woman who had entered the store's every book title and invoice number into a ledger according to a system that was unintelligible to anyone else and therefore indispensable to the business. Thus, much to Seymour's relief and their triumphant daughter-in-law's satisfaction, the decorating ended. These days, Mrs. P. contented herself with decorating the homes of "Long Island lady friends and acquaintances," spending most of her time in the designer showcase buildings along Lower Fifth Avenue, choosing glass trinkets and matching bathroom accessories for her clients. In addition to their faded designs, the Hamadans boasted four years' worth of unvacuumed book dust, to which Seymour and his white-haired secretary, but not their occasional visitors, had grown immune long ago. One ancient faded plush-covered easy chair of no recognizable color stood in a corner; to compensate for the "negative energy" coming from the overhead fluorescent lighting, the absent-minded medium had placed a reading lamp of obscure origins on a table behind the easy chair as a courteous gesture toward her boss, but Seymour, as he had once confided to Rabbi Joachim, only published books and did not read them, so the lamp went largely unused. Seymour did, however, make use of the enormous cluttered desk awkwardly placed at the center of the cubicle, from which he shouted into the telephone and dictated letters to the white-haired medium, who took notes in her own psychic shorthand, then translated them into business English before typing them on long white paper, which she collated and stacked on a wheeled iron table located directly under the glass-enclosed rare bookcase.

Rejoining the conference, Seymour's nephew noticed with some bitterness that his thoughtfulness in going upstairs and closing the store had cost him his seat. But the nephew was used to paying for his loyalty and accepted the loss, contenting himself with a disdainful curl of the lip, his trademark gesture reserved for such occasions. Besides, even if he'd chosen to drop a sarcastic comment, it would not have been heard, because the Draconian widow Mrs. Wolstein was shouting. It was her voice he'd heard at the top of the stairs drowning out all the others. And it was she, in a brightly feathered hat made of extinct birds' tails who'd leapt immediately into his vacated seat, the only comfortable one in the cubicle—the plush armchair.

With a face as gray as the rainswept streets outside, Seymour sat behind the great, cluttered desk doodling on the border of a brief *New York Times* article, many times perused, but only freshly torn from the morning edition. "Health Cure Fraud Charged to Leader of Jewish Mystical Cult," read the headline.

Mrs. Wolstein's lawyer, who had removed his raincoat to reveal what the nephew estimated to be a two-thousand-dollar (at least) custom-tailored suit, was sweating profusely. Repeatedly wiping the thick pouches of skin under his rimless eyeglasses with an oversized Belgian linen handkerchief, he was trying in vain to calm his noisy client. Leon Berkowitz, the once mild-mannered philanthropist who never spoke beyond a whisper but had unaccountably metamorphosed into a loud-mouthed tyrant since his mugging and subsequent hospital stay, was now seated on a carton stocked with recently delivered copies of the Bhagavad Gita, banging his cane on the floor for attention. Because they were all too accustomed to thinking of Berkowitz as timid, they didn't take his display of anger seriously, and no one in the room was paying attention to him. The white-haired medium, not the least put out by the cane banging—for she was accustomed to louder rapping noises from the astral plane and was, besides, slightly hard of hearing—sat at her table and took notes in psychic shorthand.

Only two people in the crush of bodies that included a generous sprinkling of the usual Priceman relatives remained silent. The first, Rabbi Mordecai Tayson, all in black, stood surveying the tumult from a small pocket of space to the left of the armchair from which the shouting Mrs. Wolstein leaned forward gesturing excitedly with both jeweled hands. The second, Sharon Berg (the last to arrive at the meeting and almost forgotten but for Seymour Priceman's last minute phone call), was squeezed shoulder to shoulder against the heavy-cheeked Priceman daughter-in-law on one side and the widow Wolstein's sweating lawyer on the other. Only one person was missing, and it was in his name that this motley group of people had assembled.

Rabbi Albert Joachim, spiritual leader of the Center for Mystical Judaism, had been unavoidably and unaccountably delayed. Bypassing Sharon, he had only a week ago sent Seymour Priceman a manila envelope from Israel containing the first of his "Clover Cure" pamphlets, written in his own fine crabbed hand, along with a letter explaining his change in plans and a request that the pamphlet be rushed into print immediately. A second manila envelope, with a London postmark, had arrived that very morning and been unceremoniously stuffed into Seymour Priceman's upper-left-hand desk drawer when Mrs. Wolstein had barged into his office unannounced. There it rested on last year's Christmas catalog of Occult Books for Special Customers at a Discount.

Although Rabbi Joachim's plans were vague, Seymour, trusting to his own intuition, had contracted with the publisher of a widely circulating health food magazine for a continuing series on Kabbalistic herbal remedies—starting with the simple clover weed. August being the slow season at his Varick Street printer, Seymour had not only managed to rush the first chapter of the series into print, but had gotten the printer to design a special edition with an exquisite lavender-colored cover. By some strange quirk—whether the printer had lavished special care on it out of boredom during the slow season, or whether by sheer chance—the book, according to Rabbi Joachim's accompanying blurb, bore about it an exotic Asian air, the ancient quintessential herbalist sort of thing people inclined to Orientalism automatically associated with the alternative healing methods of the "inscrutable Chinese." This, or indeed, perhaps the interceding spirit of Rabbi Joachim's deceased uncle himself could have been responsible for the book's maniacally successful hot-off-the-presses sales—Seymour did not presume to judge, nor to question his good fortune—for the minute his lanky clerk placed the first batch on a rotating wire book rack at the cashier's counter at the front door of the store, the "Clover Cure" pamphlets were swept up. By mid-afternoon on the second day, they were entirely out of stock, and Seymour had already placed another rush order with the printer, a larger and more ambitious one this time. On a gamble, he took out an expensive four-inch advertisement in selected spiritual magazines featuring an intentionally Oriental looking line drawing of a clover plant. By the end of the week, the latest batch of clover pamphlets was gone, too. It must be the Chinese medicine and acupuncture craze that's doing it, thought Seymour. Who am I to question?

On the following Saturday, Seymour received a call in his Brooklyn apartment. He was seated on the terrace under a striped awning watching a baseball game and scanning the latest fall book lists from England, drinking orangeade and feeling more mellow than he had in months. Mrs. Priceman was out playing mah jongg, so he'd asked the cleaning lady to please answer the phone. On taking the receiver from her, Seymour heard an unfamiliar man's voice at the other end of the line.

"Hello, this is John Davis. I'm an investigator for the Food and Drug Administration."

The man had wanted to know if he was speaking to *the* Seymour Priceman, owner of an occult bookstore located at 1432 Delancey Street in Manhattan.

Seymour at first thought it might be his belligerent nephew playing a smartass prank—he wouldn't put it past him. Pausing before answering, he said amicably, "That's me. What can I do for you, Mr. Davis?"

The investigator came right to the point.

"There's been a lawsuit lodged against Rabbi Albert Joachim, purveyor of an untested herbal remedy, by a Mrs. Ethel Wolstein. And against you, Mr. Priceman, whom she's charging for publishing Rabbi Joachim's false health care claims. I've been assigned by the criminal department of the FDA to investigate both of Mrs. Wolstein's charges."

Seymour was amazed. Some Harlem kid might be feeding on rat turds in a candy bar for five years before the FDA sent anyone to investigate. And here, only one crazy rich woman with "connections" had enough power in her arthritic pinky to ruin a lifetime's work. What was wrong with spreading around some human kindness? Since when did a little placebo effect ever hurt anybody? It certainly had helped that poor aura reader in the neck brace, a woman who might otherwise never stick her head out of her apartment in the morning. Otherwise, who knew what she might do—or not do—to herself out of loneliness?

"Are you still there?" asked the real (Seymour was sure now that it wasn't his nephew) investigator.

"Yes, I'm still here," said Seymour, his voice breaking a little. "Listen, Mr. Davis," he motioned for the cleaning lady to close the bedroom door and turn off the vacuum cleaner, but she didn't see him and he had to yell over the noise. "Why don't you come down and see me at the store on Tuesday? I haven't got anything here at home, all my materials are at my office."

"That'll be fine, Mr. Priceman. How is Tuesday morning at ten?"

"Good, we'll have coffee," Seymour said placidly, feeling stupid and lightheaded and triumphant all at once—the same feeling that came over him when he'd smoked one too many of his father's smuggled-from-Canada Cuban cigars.

Setting the phone in its cradle, he'd returned to the terrace and numbly resumed watching the ballgame. It was the top of the fourth inning, with bases loaded for the Mets, his favorite team, when Seymour panicked.

Fortunately, Mrs. Priceman had come home early and dragged him off to a party in Forest Hills. The sheer physical act entailed in driving the car and the effort to socialize with near strangers, most of them overweight and overdressed, made Seymour forget temporarily about his panic. At night, however, in his sleep, he tossed through dreams in which his store burned to the ground.

Short, wearing a shiny brown suit and brogans, John Davis looked more like a Christian book salesman from Omaha than a government inspector. But then, Seymour reasoned, how would he know what a government inspector looked like? He'd never had any business with them, never had been forced to pay off those notoriously crooked New York fire inspectors (honest Joe Banduti had come around for years and never demanded so much as a cup of coffee). Thank God he didn't own a restaurant! His uncle on his father's side had warned him away from the food business years ago.

The inspector refused the cup of coffee Seymour offered him but said he didn't mind if Seymour drank his while they talked. The sallow-faced nephew stretched his neck almost out of his collar trying to overhear what was going on in the cubicle, so Seymour got up from behind his desk and closed the door. The nephew muttered something that sounded like a question, but luckily the telephone rang then and Seymour didn't have to answer him. As he returned to his desk he heard the nephew roar something into the telephone about an "overdue bill"—he could have been threatening any one of a number of clients or business associates. From the brief snatches of conversation he heard from behind the closed door, Seymour surmised that it was a long distance call from a small bookstore in California that owed them fifteen hundred dollars for the latest shipment of the Clover Cure.

Sitting down in the plush armchair and crossing his chunky legs, Davis explained that this sort of investigation was nothing new, really—phony swamis and cancer cures abounded in these "Aquarian times."—he chuckled—as surely, being in the business of the occult, Mr. Priceman was himself aware. Mrs. Wolstein had apparently alerted the F.D.A. months before this, when a crop of Rabbi Joachim's alleged "talismans" costing her a total of one hundred and seventy-five dollars did not alleviate the "psychic disturbances" in her home.

"Considering that she's been a founding member of Rabbi Joachim's Center for Mystical Judaism from its inception, and a continuing patron, having donated more than fifty thousand dollars to date, Mrs. Wolstein is not levying these serious charges against him frivolously."

"My understanding was that the rabbi never forced anyone to buy his talismans or his books, that you only paid for those things if you felt like it—a contribution, so to speak." Seymour leaned back in his chair and cupped his ear, a habit he'd picked up from his father.

The inspector shrugged. "All I know is that she attempted back then, so she claims, to contact the party involved, namely Rabbi Albert Joachim. But it seems the only person who would talk to her was his associate, that Rabbi Tayson fellow, who stated that the Center was closed for the summer and that Rabbi Joachim had gone abroad for an indefinite length of time."

"That's right," Seymour nodded.

"As you would imagine, the news upset Mrs. Wolstein considerably. She's not the most stable person."

"That, I know. I've met her only twice, but it's obvious," said Seymour ingratiatingly, trying hard to make light of the matter.

The inspector ignored him and went on. "So she insisted on a face-to-face meeting with his associate, Rabbi Tayson."

"To whom, no doubt, she poured her heart out."

"Well," the inspector frowned at being interrupted twice, "the second-in-command himself, it seems, has been kept in the dark about most of the goings on at the Center, and when Mrs. Wolstein suggested that maybe they ought to speak with a Mrs. Berg, the Center's secretary, Rabbi Tayson told her that it would be foolish, since Mrs. Berg was fiercely involved—that's *his* word, 'fiercely'—with Rabbi Joachim, and with his schemes, too, so Mrs. Berg scarcely could be expected to be reliable."

Davis stopped for breath, cleared his throat and resumed in a more official tone. "According to the complainant, Rabbi Tayson appeared to be genuinely unaware of the quackery going on under his nose, so to speak, and, because he was unwilling, he said, to lend his name to it any further, he told Mrs. Wolstein that he would join forces with her in exposing Rabbi Joachim as a fake. Rabbi Tayson then agreed to undertake an internal investigation of the Center's activities himself."

"Oh?"

"And he hadn't gotten very far when the Clover Cure pamphlet was dropped, so to speak, into his lap. On the advice of Mrs. Wolstein's attorney, Rabbi Tayson telephoned our district branch asking for tests of the medicinal properties of the plant. And that's where you—as the publisher of the book—come in, isn't it, Mr. Priceman?" Davis smiled good-naturedly, simultaneously tugging at his socks.

The inspector went on to tell Seymour that it was Mrs. Wolstein, through her late husband's cousin, a publicity agent, who telephoned (prematurely, in Davis's opinion) the *New York Times* about the story, and asked her attorney to file a lawsuit against Rabbi Joachim and the Center for Mystical Judaism for marketing an unproven cure for addiction and other mental disturbances, and against Seymour Priceman, for publishing Rabbi Joachim's false claims.

"To put it bluntly, it was Mrs. Wolstein's idea to make a stink about it. Rabbi Tayson strikes me as the quiet type; he doesn't want any publicity at all."

According to Davis, several additional claims were made, none of which could be proven. Besides, those complaints were under the jurisdiction of the vice squad, not the FDA. But, Davis confided, leaning forward in his chair, being a man of the world, Seymour Priceman could easily guess what kinds of complaints he was talking about: "the usual sordid accusations relating to so-called gurus and 'spiritual teachers' like Rabbi Joachim, hanky-panky, the blond divorcée secretary, the way-with-the-ladies sort of thing that's so common with these guys, the flashy car, even the misappropriation of funds designated by a contributor named Leon Berkowitz for the construction of a new building for the Center in Los Angeles that never got built. It's your typical religious scandal, a pit without a bottom, so to speak."

Placing his hands on his knees under the desk, Seymour clenched and unclenched his fists. Two hours later, Mrs. Wolstein's sweating attorney was standing in front of him at that same desk, addressing the assembled interested parties.

"Of course, there's the real possibility that your Rabbi Joachim has flown the coop, left you all holding the bag—if you'll pardon me for mixing metaphors."

Seymour doubted that. Something inside told him that Albert Joachim would return. He'd doubted him briefly on Saturday, but not any longer, and was now determined to stick by him—whatever happened. Not because he believed in Rabbi Joachim's hocus-pocus, but because Tayson, that self-serving son-of-a-bitch, had so quickly abandoned his mentor and joined the attack. Partly, too, Seymour was thinking, because aligning himself with quixotic types came naturally to him. He would back Albert Joachim for what he, Seymour, knew to be the Kabbalah master's sincere and crazy (if misdirected) desire to repair the broken world. And partly, too, for the sake of Sharon Berg, who had been targeted by the venomous Rabbi Tayson as Albert Joachim's mistress, and co-conspirator, in the hope that she would take the rap for the Center's operations. Though he was usually not a vengeful person, there lingered in a far corner of Seymour's mind the savor of taking a little revenge against both the quisling Rabbi Tayson and the vicious Mrs. Wolstein.

"He's got to be nuts if he thinks he's going to get away with this," interjected Seymour's nephew, wringing his hands. But his comment was drowned out by a new round of invective from Mrs. Wolstein.

The white-haired medium noted down every word, including the curses.

Seymour briefly considered that the widow might have been drinking, then returned to his own thoughts.

Sharon understood little of what was going on around her. The cubicle was sweltering, Mrs. Wolstein, whom she had never again expected to meet, was eyeing her malevolently. Charges were being flung at her, at the Center, at Seymour Priceman, who had called Sharon early that morning. Paulie had been feverish and she'd planned to stay home. She was still recovering from the weekend. Seymour had hurriedly mentioned an emergency, something having to do with Rabbi Joachim. The kitchen had turned upside down as she'd rocked against a cupboard holding her hand to her head.

"His plane crashed? He's dead?" she'd screamed into the telephone.

"No, no, no, don't be so morbid. He's fine. I just got a letter from him. He won't be back for a while yet."

Seymour Priceman had a letter—and as Sharon listened to the details, she felt her relief turn to rage. Rabbi Joachim might just as well have crashed for all she cared. Once again, he'd passed her by, as if she were invisible, a cipher, a nonentity. Grandiose dreams were all he'd left her with, lost among the clover-covered cliffs of the Jersey Palisades. It was funny, the way she'd impulsively spilled out her story to Junior Cantana while they were driving back from Pennsylvania. No, not funny, laughable, the way she'd rambled on about her devotion to Rabbi Joachim, her Kabbalah master, who, despite the fact that she was a woman, and therefore forbidden to practice, had welcomed her into his sanctuary as his disciple and confidante, offering her the chance of someday proving herself worthy of receiving his transmission of spiritual power. How she'd betrayed her master's trust by getting involved with him, a gentile, and even worse, how she'd sullied the code of chastity demanded of all Kabbalists by engaging in sex with him.

Junior didn't say a word, didn't even try to take her hand and offer comfort, remaining silent until he pulled the car up to her house. Only when he'd taken out her bag and carried it to her front door, did he say, "Let me think about this. I'll call you." Then turning from her he'd walked away without looking back.

"No, never! Never call me again!" she'd screamed.

The green bag still lay unopened in a corner of the foyer.

Standing in Seymour's office, Sharon wondered whether, if he were there, Rabbi Joachim would have noticed that she was not wearing stockings. Whether, if Rabbi Joachim, and not Seymour Priceman, had been sitting behind the big desk looking at her sadly, he would have seen through her unkempt exterior, smelled the weekend's sex on her regardless of the hours she'd spent trying to wash it away. Would he have given

her the gift he'd brought her anyway? It would be just like him to con-
fuse her by giving her a reward: a bag of Israeli apricots plucked from his
jacket pocket, fresh and unspoiled despite much traveling. Moist and
sweet. Flung like an afterthought in front of her on Priceman's desk.

But there were no apricots, and Rabbi Joachim wasn't coming
back. Not if she was to believe the wildly gesticulating Mrs. Wolstein.
Not ever. He was a fraud. A crook. A seducer. Sharon laughed bitterly
to herself. Though everyone expected it of her, she did not say a word
to defend him. How could she—the rabbi's indispensable secretary,
sharer of his mystical secrets, recorder of his plans—stand there and
remain silent against the accusations flying all around her? What
secrets? Sharon knew nothing about Rabbi Joachim at all. Nothing,
except for her own desperate, unreturned love. She'd spent all that time
reveling in her pain until it had been wrested from her by strangers.
Now, even the newspapers were flaunting it.

"Quiet, everyone," Seymour Priceman startled the group into
silence. "We'll accomplish nothing this way, except for sore throats
and," he crooked an eyebrow in the direction of his nephew, "ulcers."

Mrs. Wolstein's lawyer looked around for a seat. Finding none,
he set his briefcase on the floor and sat down on it. Eyeing his watch,
Rabbi Tayson edged toward the door. The widow collapsed in her
chair, mascara streaking her wrinkled, tear-stained cheeks.

"I suggest everyone clear out but Mrs. Berg," continued Seymour.
"I'll explain everything to her from the beginning, and maybe then
we'll learn what's really happening here."

The industrious medium moistened her pencil with the tip of her
tongue and turned the page.

A Tibetan mandala featuring a bevy of multicolored, multi-limbed
demons Sharon hadn't noticed before glared at her from a poster on
the wall behind Seymour's desk. One of them danced on six legs as

it flung human skulls into a cauldron. Sharon felt faint but quickly recovered at the thought of Paulie sick at home. But she didn't want to think of home because Junior Cantana kept calling, and Pinnie was starting to complain about having to answer and make excuses for why Sharon couldn't talk to him. No peace at home. No peace anywhere. Not since she had brought the goy—the stranger—into her life to tamper with Rabbi Joachim's secrets. Now she was being punished, publicly exposed and humiliated.

"What for?" asked Seymour's insolent nephew. "Anything she has to say should be heard by all of us. We're all involved in this, considering we're all liable."

The nephew's outburst was followed by further confusion about the extent and degree of each participant's culpability or innocence in the matter. This time, Mrs. Wolstein's lawyer did not join the discussion but sat on his upturned briefcase pondering the conflicting arguments being made around him. Granted, Priceman was an interested party and—intentionally or not—was on Rabbi Joachim's side. He was eager to hear what the blond secretary had to say. So far, she'd said nothing, which was odd. She'd just stood around looking glassy-eyed the whole time. He'd seen witnesses like her before, people with plenty of valuable information who were too dazed to testify in anyone's behalf. But given a little coaxing, assured that she had a *friend*—she was sure to come around. Mistresses, especially those who'd been cast aside, always did. (In addition to his J.D., the lawyer had a master's degree in psychology.) This woman was definitely unstable, ready to break down. Thin, rangy, big hands and long legs, not very delicate features—something almost mannish about her. Probably wild in bed, though. The religious ones always were.

"I agree with Mr. Priceman," Mrs. Wolstein's lawyer said, rising from his seat on the briefcase. "Mrs. Berg was dragged in here at the last minute; nobody told her what was really going on. It's obvious that she's upset—"

"What about me? I'm upset, too," wailed Mrs. Wolstein.

Restraining the impulse to throw a sheaf of loose bills in her face, Seymour covered his eyes with his hands instead.

Rabbi Tayson, meanwhile, had quietly slipped out of the office during the heated exchange.

Ignoring his client, the lawyer assumed his most fatherly manner and, looking straight at Sharon, said, "This young lady here is equally entitled to advice from counsel. She did come on the scene a little late—"

"Of course," the medium piped up in her tiny bird-voice. "This isn't France, where they presume everyone guilty before proven innocent. This is America."

Seymour's daughter-in-law vigorously nodded her head in agreement.

"What say you give us an hour?" Seymour said reasonably.

"I'll second that," said Leon Berkowitz. His weak leg was tight with sitting so long, and he desperately longed to stand up. Besides, his newly acquired tyrannical air had worn off. Since he much preferred Rabbi Joachim's company to the widow's, and since money came so easily to him anyway, Mr. Berkowitz really didn't mind so much that the Kabbalah master might have taken off with five thousand dollars from the Center's account. Even more important, detesting publicity of any kind, Mr. Berkowitz was now truly sorry that he'd let himself be so hastily enlisted in the Widow Wolstein's crusade against the Center for Mystical Judaism. He would have much preferred to call Rabbi Joachim long distance and have the whole thing out with him person-to-person by telephone. Unfortunately, no one seemed to know where Rabbi Joachim was.

The office was cleared. Receiving Seymour's thanks for her services, even the medium left, and a reluctant Mrs. Wolstein, invited to lunch at Priceman's expense, was tactfully ushered into a nearby delicatessen.

Left alone, Sharon and Seymour now faced each other—she diffidently, he with a head full of questions. What did one say to a woman who was madly in love with a man who didn't know she loved him—or if he did, didn't care? Worse yet, what did one say to said woman when she'd been abandoned by said man and left to answer for his questionable business practices?

Seymour let out a long sigh. Then he pointed to the armchair and said, "Take a seat, Sharon. You've been standing for an hour."

Sharon sat down. The armchair was still warm and scented by Mrs. Wolstein's heavy lilac perfume.

Seymour picked up the telephone and buzzed the one upstairs clerk, a lanky college boy who did him favors without complaining.

"Hello, Mel? Would you run across the street to the Italians like a good fella and order me two hero sandwiches." Cupping the receiver against his shirt, he whispered to Sharon, "What do you want—cheese? Ham? The works?"

"No ham," Sharon said, realizing that those were the first words she'd uttered since entering Seymour's office an hour ago.

"Coke or coffee?"

"Tea, please."

"They have everything," Seymour said. Then, brushing an imaginary fly from his papers, he removed the receiver from his chest and shouted into it. "Mel? You still there? Good. Here's the order: one pepperoni hero with the works and very hot coffee, black. And one cheese hero, no meat, and tea—lemon or milk?" he asked Sharon, this time without bothering to cover the telephone's mouthpiece.

"Lemon."

"Make that tea with lemon. I'll consider you for a ten-day holiday next Christmas instead of the usual week."

Mel's gleeful shouts could be heard from the other end of the wire.

"Like fun, I will," said Seymour, putting his hand over the receiver and winking at Sharon. It crossed his mind as he spoke that nothing could be that bad as long as you were in good health, which—despite the imagined circulation problems—he was. Knock wood. Then removing his hand from the receiver, he said, "Okay, Mel, I'll pay you back when you come down. What's that? Sure I'll give you a tip—the tip of my shoe, now get going. I've got an important hungry customer waiting here." Seymour replaced the telephone in its cradle and said, "Mel's a good kid; he's working his way through Cooper Union, wants to be an engineer. Now all he needs is a girlfriend; know anyone nice?"

Sharon started to cry.

Always awkward in the face of a woman's tears, Seymour sat playing cat's cradle with a rubber band until it snapped. Then he shoved a box of tissues toward her. Inwardly, he sighed—more for Sharon than for himself. What did it matter as far as the business was concerned? So he'd learned his lesson not to trust every maniac who came in off the streets with deals. Still, he'd go on doing favors; he was constituted that way. Partially, it was his fault; he wasn't trying to pawn it off on anyone else. How long could a publisher get away with printing material that he'd never read? Who reads such stuff, anyway, he wondered. Women like this one, I'll bet. Having answered his own question satisfactorily, Seymour swiveled from left to right in his creaky leather chair.

"Tell me something, Sharon," do you really believe in all this?" He pointed to the book-lined walls with a pudgy, ink-stained finger.

Sharon looked up at Seymour in surprise. She was in the midst of blowing her nose with one of his tissues and couldn't answer him right away.

"I don't know," she said at last, restraining further sobs.

"What do you mean, you don't know? You either believe in it or you don't," Seymour said, his tone indicating that he was slightly exasperated with her as well as sympathetic. "I got people upstairs who spend every spare penny on these books, and whatever is left over from that they put down on initiation fees to gurus, swamis, yogis, and Kabbalah masters like your Rabbi Joachim. Now *that's* what I call believing."

Sharon looked up at him again. Her eyes and nose were red. "Do you happen to have a cigarette, Mr. Priceman?"

"Seymour," he corrected, rummaging through a drawer and coming up with a rumpled pack of Salems. "Mentholated only, and probably stale."

"I'll take one."

Although he did not smoke, Priceman carried a very expensive opal lighter with him, a well-intended gift from a grateful congregation of an Ocean Parkway synagogue, where he'd lectured without a fee on "The Popularity of Occultism among Jewish Youth". The flame danced between them, nearly singeing Sharon's eyelashes as she lit up.

"Sorry, too much lighter fluid." Seymour drew himself up in his chair, then leaned back and put his feet up, resting his clumsy orthopedic shoes on the desk. "Ugly shoes, no?"

Sharon nodded.

"You don't have to agree with everything I say, you know."

"Sorry."

"Ah, now she's sorry. Listen, kid, you have a mind of your own. Or don't you? I mean, how can anyone your age be so naïve? Or is it an act?" Then, in an afterthought, "What are you, about thirty, thirty-five?"

Sharon's lip began to tremble.

Okay, so he'd been too harsh and gone too far too quickly. Time to retreat. Seymour wished he hadn't volunteered to talk to Sharon about her relationship with Rabbi Joachim. This was a delicate issue, and what did he know of love? He'd been married to Mrs. P. for twenty-seven years. She went her way and he went his. Seymour was married to the store, Mrs. P. said. "The store is your mink coat and your New Year's vacation in Florida," he replied. As for the goods he peddled—well, at least it wasn't pornography—he'd settled that issue with his conscience long ago.

"There's good and bad in everything," Seymour said, as much to Sharon as to himself. "People take what they need; it all depends on your level of development." Now where had he picked that one up? It must have been from the medium, a confirmed believer in reincarnation, who told Seymour he'd been a Tibetan brigand in a former life, assuring him afterward that owning the bookstore was an advance in his "karmic level of development." Watch it, Seymour, he thought, or you'll be buying this stuff yourself soon.

The food arrived then. Crushing her cigarette in the ashtray Seymour had provided, Sharon unwrapped her sandwich and began eating greedily. The hero was bathed in olive oil and slathered with mustard and covered with hot red cherry peppers, onions, and shredded lettuce, and was delicious. It would destroy her stomach later, especially since she hadn't eaten a full meal since the Purple Hen—and that was four days ago. But she was hungry, famished, and the hot, spicy food tasted good to her now. She took a sip of watery tea and burned her tongue. The paper tag of the tea bag fell into the cup.

Seymour took a bite of his sandwich. As he sat watching Sharon trying to fish the paper tag out of her cup with the wooden stirrer, Seymour decided to level with her. Years of experience dealing with harmless lunatics now lent him the confidence he'd been lacking a few minutes ago. Best was to give it to her straight. That had been his motto when customers came to him for advice about business deals, divorces, and changes of residence. Maybe the years he'd spent at Priceman's had also rubbed off some of their "occult" wisdom on his shoulders. Why else would he be sought after as a home-grown oracle, a neighborhood sphinx, if his customers didn't assume that being surrounded by all that arcana all those years had made him wise? Sometimes, although he would never admit it to anyone, even Seymour himself believed this to be true.

Being honest in his advice had cost him nothing. On the contrary, it had gained him friends and many influential customers. And he had only been robbed once in fifteen years—non-violently—by a stock clerk. If a college kid wanted to buy what Seymour considered to be a "bad" book, or a "drug" book, he would say, "It's junk, I don't carry it." Pointing to a rear shelf, he'd add that so-and-so had written something more interesting on the same subject—even if he didn't read it, Seymour knew his stock inside out—and he'd sell the kid a book that would keep him away from trouble. Word got around that he was honest and dependable. Soon even the astrologers and magicians were asking him for advice. He had "positive energy," they said.

Once, when two ten-year-old boys came all the way from Staten Island to buy an expensive phony magic book, he'd sold them a cheaper, secondhand one with better illustrations written by a famous magician who debunked phonies. Claiming he didn't need the stuff lying around the store, Seymour had thrown in a sleight-of-hand deck of cards and a magic wand for free. Seymour was "cool," the kids said. Ah, but kids were different. They filled in the gaps for themselves. Not like the poor woman sitting in front of him, still fishing for the paper tag in her teacup. She was no kid, and he, Seymour, was obliged to treat her like a grownup, set her straight before she got herself into *real* trouble.

"I'll ask you again. Do you really believe in all this?" Seymour pointed his finger directly at Rabbi Joachim's Zohar.

Sharon put down her teacup and looked him in the eye. "I love him," she said quietly and simply.

That's nice, Seymour thought, dumping too much sugar into his coffee, very nice. No use mincing words. It was time to talk, and talk fast. In twenty minutes the enemy would return. John Davis had promised another visit tomorrow. Someone from the *Times* had been trying to reach him on the telephone all morning—for a follow-up story, no doubt. And Seymour's printer was threatening to come to the store and commit suicide in front of all the customers on the main floor.

Dismissing all sentiment with a wave of his stirrer, Seymour said, "I don't mean to sound harsh, but that has nothing to do with this problem right here," knowing, of course, that it had everything to do with it. "I love Rabbi Joachim too, in my own way, and he's gotten us both into hot water. Granted, he's charming, enigmatic, charismatic, even. A regular misunderstood hero. But where does that leave *us*, Sharon? Me, I never believed a word of his program." Seymour took a gulp of his coffee and smacked his lips. Too sweet, but he needed a heavy dose of sugar now. "Of course Rabbi Joachim believes it; in fact, I would go so far as to say that he's never had any intention of putting anything over on us."

"Whoever said that he wanted to fool anyone?" Bristling at the challenge Seymour had thrown her, Sharon stopped fussing with the teabag, put aside her sandwich, and placed both hands on the desk. Beneath the tears there now lurked anger. And beneath the anger, a tiny ray of hope that she might see Rabbi Joachim again.

"Oh, nobody—just all those people we got rid of a few minutes ago who were crying for his head, just the *New York Times*, the Food and Drug Administration, and soon, maybe even Nader's Raiders." Seymour's face turned beet red with annoyance. That was not it, not the right way. He calmed himself, then, indicating the drawer containing Rabbi Joachim's letter, he said, "There's a letter from him here. I told you about it this morning. Of course there's no return address, but it's postmarked Tel Aviv," he lied, "and let me tell you now, Sharon, that if you know anything about Rabbi Joachim's secret files, you'd better give them to me right away. Tayson has ransacked the Center's office; he's way ahead of us already. And you're next. That snazzy lawyer is sure to subpoena your personal files. But listen to me, I'm on your side. I figure our Rabbi Joachim really believes in that dead uncle of his. And for all I know, maybe he's full of 'divine light' or whatever he calls it. But as he told me so himself, right here in this office, he never has and never will give any guarantees or promises— to anyone. That's why I took him on in the first place. He's harmless; he just tells his disciples to work things out for themselves, that's all. If they're sincere, he says, if they practice his 'meditations' or pray a little—what have you—they're entitled to 'enlightenment.' Don't ask me what that means; I have no idea. I suspect Rabbi Joachim thinks he's been entrusted by his uncle with the answers to life and death. So what if you don't get enlightened after ten easy lessons, so you've lost only a few bucks and stood to gather some good deeds along the way. And he never promised anyone—at least not to my knowledge—that they'd be 'cured' by drinking clover tea, either. So there's the whole thing in a nutshell." Seymour clapped his hands. "If our Kabbalah master is a phony, at least he's not an intentional one, because he guarantees you nothing. And that's why they won't get him. Love him or not, lady, it's you and me who are going to be left 'holding the bag,' as our lawyer friend phrased it so aptly."

Silence.

Seymour watched the second hand on his desk clock rotate across the face with astonishing speed. Determined to hold his assault, he made a show of forming the greasy sandwich wrappings into miniature basketballs and tossed them into his wastebasket a few feet away. One "ball" made a direct hit; the other two tapped the rim and rolled off sluggishly onto the floor.

"I have no personal secret files, Seymour, I swear it."

Sharon's dismal whine convinced him that she was being insincere. Okay, then, he'd let her have the truth right between the eyes. This one didn't deserve the kid gloves treatment.

"What about the astrologer? Didn't you know that Rabbi Joachim regularly consulted an astrologer, one of my own very best and oldest customers? What kind of superman is that, what kind of psychic powers? Did you also *not* know that he came to see her about two weeks before he left New York, asking her for a reading? He was very upset, and she told him that it would be a very 'propitious time' for a trip to Israel. Do you know why?" The hurried catechism left Seymour breathless. His heart pounding, he paused for air.

Sharon frowned. An astrologer? What was this all about? Seymour was trying to discredit Rabbi Joachim—that was it. He was launching a cheap shot just to wrench some sordid confession from her. Trying to remain cool, she said, "I thought such information was confidential. Can't the astrologer be sued for telling you?" she asked.

Seymour looked at her angrily for the first time but said nothing. Sharon had spoken effortlessly. It was as if Rabbi Joachim himself was putting the words in her mouth, at the same time enclosing her in a calm, serene glow of expectation, even approaching joy. She had the upper hand. Now it was her turn to crumple the leftover papers into miniature basketballs and toss them into the wastebasket—all three of her tosses accurately finding their mark. She could barely keep from smiling.

Seymour saw his golden moment. Sharon was sitting smugly back in her chair, vulnerable, an open target.

"Rabbi Joachim told me himself," he told Sharon. "*He* told me, not the astrologer. How about the fact that the real reason for his trip was to get a divorce from his wife? Did you know *that*? Or that he's been in the process of divorcing for nearly six months because the wife wouldn't allow him visiting rights with his kids? How does *that* one hit you?"

Sharon's poor battered heart leapt like a bird breaking through the icy trees in its first flight toward spring. She longed to jump up from her chair and hug Seymour for telling her this, knew instinctively that it was true, that he was not merely prodding her for information but that in his desperation he was telling her everything Rabbi Joachim had made him swear to reveal to her only when the time was right. And the time was right now! Now!

"I—I knew it, but I wasn't supposed to tell anyone," Sharon murmured, gathering confidence as she went along.

Now it was Seymour's turn to be surprised. "So we both know," he could barely keep himself from shouting. It was two minutes to twelve. "So now, what?"

Overhead, Sharon heard the bustle of the returning combatants. No longer afraid, certain that Rabbi Joachim was guiding her, she burst out, "He's going to marry *me*. I've known it all along. The Center is closed. I closed it myself when he left."

It was twelve o'clock. Mrs. Wolstein could be heard wheezing her way downstairs. Mr. Berkowitz was tapping his cane against the closed office door.

SEVENTEEN

Time is a joke. Time is a paradox. Time is.

—Anonymous

IT WAS SHARON'S BIRTHDAY, THE SEVENTH SATURDAY after the Fourth of July, 1972. The Coney Island sky was overcast, the air gray, soft and humid, and the low-lying clouds fairly tumescent with rain. Not really a day for a walk along the beach; hardly a short fresh breeze from the water, where now even the waves seemed to hang back, creating a stagnant pond skimmed by beer cans, ice cream wrappers, orange rinds, and the thousand-and-one varieties of summer detritus from the city. A day when the curly-headed boys in sneakers were out in full force, flitting through the traffic on Stillwell Avenue with rags at the ready, attacking windshields. A black priest made his way down the street toward a yellow brick church to deliver Communion in Creole to his Haitian congregation. A homeless couple wrapped in a blanket slept with their arms around each other in the doorway of an empty store. This was not a place for lovers.

An old man sat on a bench on the boardwalk clasping his hat in his hands. His legs were spread out in front of him, making it impossible for anyone to pass between him and the guardrail. Inside his wind-breaker, he carried a black jack in the hope of staving off a mugging. He was watching the young couple on the neighboring bench, studying their body language to see if they were dangerous or not. Deciding they were not, he placed his hat over his face and pretended to sleep while peering out from under it. Though he thought of himself as tough, the old man (who was once a sailor) was still soft when it came to love.

"You know what you ought to do," the young man was saying to the woman, "you ought to stay with me. " His hair was uncombed and he looked as if he'd slept in his khaki army field jacket. The woman was older than her partner, blond and too skinny for the old man's taste. She didn't say anything, just sat there, staring, off in her own world.

"Stay with me," urged the young man.

Suddenly, the woman spoke. "I didn't know they kept the Whip closed all summer. I loved that ride better than all the rest. Arleen pre-ferred the roller coaster, but it used to make me sick to my stomach." The woman sounded like she might be drunk, or on drugs.

"Stay with me," pleaded the young man. It was as if he were singing a song, sad, yet pleasing to the old man.

"Thank you for the corn and the root beer," said the woman. "I really shouldn't be eating anything at Nathan's. It's not Kosher, you know."

"Don't throw your life away, Sharon. Come with me. Bring Paulie, bring Phyllis, you can even bring your mother if you want to. We'll live out in the country, and there'll be room enough for everyone."

"I told you not to call me. Why did you call me when I told you not to? And then bursting into my house unannounced, scaring the children," the woman chided listlessly.

"I told your mother I was coming; I didn't burst," the young man couldn't go on any longer. Slumping heavily against the bench, he started sobbing.

"I can't—I can't. Oh, please don't cry, I can't take it when you cry, please stop!"

"Sharon, dearest, why are you doing this? Why?"

"Don't you see? It's because I love him, even if he isn't really what he claimed to be. Even if he took off without telling me, I believe in him. I believe that he's coming back to me someday. Maybe not this year or the next, but he'll be back. He's divorced his wife."

"How can you? He's gone, vanished from your life. He never cared for you. You almost landed in jail trying to cover up for him. You'll wreck yourself and your kids if you go looking for him."

Moving away from her rejected lover, the woman started to get up from the bench then changed her mind and sat down again. Out in the water, the foghorn of a flat-snout tanker tooted three times. A girl screamed as the Parachute descended toward the boardwalk.

It had gotten hotter. The invisible, milky sun was directly overhead. The old man's woolen hat felt scratchy against his face. He wished he'd brought his pipe with him; he could have used a smoke now.

The young man caught his breath in a sob, but it was the woman who spoke, this time rapidly, with excitement. "It isn't what you believe in that counts, it's that you believe in something instead of just floating around aimlessly until you die. I had nothing until I came to know him—nothing! And without him, I'll stay nothing. Why can't you understand that? Why is it so hard? It's so clear to me. Why doesn't anyone understand? You believe in your drawing, in your art. Icaro believes in saving the poor. Seymour Priceman, Rabbi Joachim's publisher, believes in his business. Why can't you let *me* have something to believe in?"

"I love you, Sharon. I'd give up everything and become whatever you wanted. We could have a life together, go somewhere far from here. You could go back to school if you wanted to—anything!"

"Oh, leave me alone, please!" the woman wailed, startling the old man, and he jumped, his hat sliding down from his face onto his chest. Now that he had an unobstructed view of what was going on, he no longer pretended to be sleeping.

"Come to me, Sharon. Just let me hold you a while. Let's stop talking, just for a little bit." The young man had stopped crying and was gently coaxing the woman to come closer.

The old man smelled frying onions. He'd forgotten about being hungry and was totally immersed in the couple's bittersweet drama. Though he'd long since abandoned the joys and pangs of love. Protected by a heavy layer of scars so old and faded they no longer hurt him even a little, he found it strangely pleasant to relive them now.

The woman wrenched herself free of her lover's grasp. As she got to her feet, the old man's hat slithered from his chest to the boardwalk floor.

"Stay with me," pleaded the handsome young man in the army field jacket. "Where are you going?"

"To the Parachute." The woman was walking away, her voice ringing shrilly against the open expanse of sky and the easy lapping of the waves. "Let's take a ride on the Parachute."

Her lover got up from the bench.

Reaching down for his hat, the old man felt a sharp pain in his chest.

"Wait!"

The woman was already approaching the entrance to the Parachute as her lover caught up with her.

It always happens that way with women when they make up their minds to do something crazy, thought the old man, retrieving his hat. As soon as he sat upright again the pain in his chest disappeared.

"I want to ride it once before it closes for the season," the woman called out. "I've never ridden it in my life, I've always been too afraid, but I'm not afraid now!"

THE KABBALAH MASTER

"Ha!" the old man exploded. Disgusted with the way the drama was ending, he hacked up a blob of phlegm and spat it out on the boardwalk. Looking up, he saw that the young man had caught up with his sweetheart and that the two of them were walking arm in arm toward the doggone Parachute. This made the old man want to spit again, but his store of phlegm was exhausted. Feeling under his windbreaker for his trusty black jack, he got up from the bench and trudged solemnly back to his room at the Old Sailor's Home.

* * *

RABBI JOACHIM WAS COMING BACK FOR HER, Sharon was sure of it. And if he wasn't coming back, it was because he wanted her to fly to him. Ascending, as she was now to join him in the misty upper regions. On the boardwalk below, small as an ant, an old man limped away, taking her fear with him, and Sharon laughed out loud. The Parachute creaked and bumped its way upward, faster now. Junior Cantana was sitting next to her, already forgotten, replaced by the rushing wind in her ears and the faraway roar of the white-capped sea. She was soaring alone—a divine being with flaming hair, ascending toward the Kabbalah master who had been testing her all along—her loyalty, her mettle, her capacity to withstand all the world's lies. It was he who had created the entire illusory summer, gathering all the people, perhaps even playing all the parts himself: Jorge Diaz, to scare her; Officer Pols, to protect her; Junior Cantana, to tempt her; Rabbi Tayson, to betray her—even George Kellner, her father, to teach her how to love. Rabbi Joachim had played them all for her, whipping off one mask and replacing it with another. To think she'd doubted him for even a minute! How stupid of her not to have seen it before!

199

Now no longer cowering and trembling before him, Sharon had reached the last stage in her initiation. The distant roaring in her ears suddenly turned into laughter. The sun burned with it. The sea danced with it. The sky resounded with it. The great belly of God shook with it.

Of course Rabbi Joachim would come back for her. Didn't he always?

ACKNOWLEDGMENTS

Thank you to my publisher, Paul Cohen, a sincere spiritual seeker in his own right, and to the staff at Monkfish Book Publishing Company for their efforts in making my book as lovely as I would have wished.

To my friends and family, forgive me for not listing you by name, but accept a deep gassho for your loyalty and excellent insights into my work.

Thank you to the late Rabbis Zvi Yehudah Kook, Aryeh Kaplan, Zalman Schachter-Shalomi, and Shlomo Carlebach, and to Madame Colette Aboulker Muscat, and all the real and imagined Kabbalah masters past, present, and future.

But thank you most of all, to Manfred Steger, my husband, spiritual partner, collaborator, and soul mate, for inspiring me to soar.

CPSIA information can be obtained
at www.ICGtesting.com
Printed in the USA
LVOW03s1354130418
573311LV00001B/1/P